I0551797

Confessions of a

Failed Yuppie

A novel

Patricia Parsons

ISBN 978-0-9685456-3-8 (paperback)

Cover image credit: Natashok/Dreamstime.com

"YUPPIE"
A Definition

Acronym for <u>Y</u>oung <u>U</u>rban <u>P</u>rofessional, usually occurring in a married pair (often male/female but not necessarily). Categorized as upper middle class or at least moving in that direction, ambitious, well-educated. Characterized by excessive concerns about appearances. Lightly narcissistic. May have money or at least leverage. But not necessarily. Normal habitat is the urban condo, sometimes the single-family dwelling of dubious heritage in a downtown area with a postage stamp for a yard, for which a bidding war took place prior to acquisition. Yuppies with children often move to larger, more impressive dwellings. Diet consists mainly of cocktails, organic kale and the latest gastronomic fad. Would not be caught dead in a North-American-produced automobile brand. Skis in winter, does hot yoga, plays squash (it's making a come-back), and quietly brags all year round. Widely thought to have become extinct in the early 1990's. Not so much.

Confessions of a Failed Yuppie

PROLOGUE

Every once in a while I spot something, hear a familiar snippet of music or smell something that reminds me of how far I've come in such a short time. In fact, it's just two years by my count. Just this morning I spotted a black Porsche with one of those yellow diamond patches on the rear window. You know the ones. They say all kinds of strange things. This one said "baby on board." As if! Do you realize how ridiculous that is on the back of a Porsche Carrera? Imagine trying to get one of those gargantuan car seats that parents seem to think will protect their little ones in the event of a terrorist attack into the back seat of that car. Oh, I forgot, Porsche Carrera's don't have back seats. Anyway, it was this seemingly innocuous occurrence in my life that brought back memories of the difference between where I was two years ago, and where I am now.

As we speak (I guess I'm really the only one speaking right now), I am on the cusp of my fortieth birthday. A monumental event some might say. I am actually quite happy and serene now, but that wasn't always the case. In fact, just over two years ago, I was in what you might call "a bit of a state."

1

I was the embodiment of a fraud, trying to bluff my way through a life that I knew drove my friends onward and upward, but that just made me stressed and frustrated. I was never able to put my finger on why at the time, but as I look back, I have the benefit of that 20/20 hindsight.

Whenever I visited my mother to bemoan my very existence, she told me to 'have your head examined' her usual way of telling me that I was an idiot. After all, who wouldn't love my life? Me?

My husband, who can (thankfully) no longer claim that title, thought I was entirely too intense for my own good. He was always telling me to 'chill.' Just chill, Jill, he'd say and then he'd laugh in that endearingly snorting kind of way he had. My name is not Jill. Can you see my eyes rolling? Trust me, they are. What the heck does someone who spends every working hour with his hands inside someone's mouth know anyway? The truth is that my mother and my now-ex-husband were both wrong about me.

I was simply suffering from what is rapidly becoming what I believe to be increasingly common although rarely admitted malady. In fact, most sufferers are as unlikely to admit to having this affliction as they are to having herpes. Having now completely recovered, I am not afraid to say it: I am a failed Yuppie.

I can hear the Yuppies –and the aspiring Yuppies – choking on their organic kimchee while reaching for a glass of biodynamic wine. To think that one of the chosen few (or many depending on who is counting) would come right out and say something so heinous is unthinkable. I think I'm supposed to just quietly fade away in an effort to ensure that I do not disturb anyone else's fragile world. The Yuppie motto might well be, "Don't rock the boat."

I cannot now pinpoint the exact day when I knew that something was amiss in my perfect life. I seemed to be doing all the right things. I was certainly urban, and I was a professional. Check. Check. I was, or should I say we were upwardly mobile. In fact, I even had a secret source of income that not even my dear husband knew about, but I'll get to that, and since it was a secret from just about everyone (it was just one of those little secrets that wives keep between themselves and their wealth managers), I don't think it really affected anything.

We lived in an urban, reclaimed row house on a recently gentrified downtown street around the corner from an outrageously expensive purveyor of organic foods and wines. (Did I mention the biodynamic fad?). We had renovated that three-story stacked house within an inch of its life: there were gleaming hardwood floors that evidently gave off no gases; there was granite on the counter tops; there was a low-flow, rain shower head in the shower out of which trickled a light rain shower resulting the need for me to spend 15 minutes under it every morning in a vain attempt to get the shampoo out of my hair; there was a BMW in the driveway – my husband's I have to say up front – and a maid service that came in once a week with their non-toxic, non-chemical cleaning supplies leaving the place smelling of vinegar such that I always thought someone was cooking fish and chips for dinner. Oh, of course there was the refrigerator set at a constant 37 degrees centigrade to ensure that our organic vegetables that every week cost me as much as one year of university tuition had back in the day would stay as tasty as the day they were picked – and I couldn't taste the difference. Did everyone think that they were going to live forever? In my view, everyone has to die from something – I for one wanted to enjoy myself on the way.

I owned a microwave convection oven whose convection activity never did make any sense to me. I shopped at all the smart downtown boutiques, and my closet bulged with minor designers and over 60 pairs of shoes. Even my mother commented several times on the fact that I have only two feet and can wear only two shoes at any one time – but I digress. I do remember lying once or twice to friends about

4

my ventures to suburban malls where I liked to troll the shops where normal people shopped. That was before it started to get trendy to "buy low," so to speak. Of course that was before everyone started to boycott the cheap stores because of the working conditions in Sri Lanka and beyond. It was hard to keep up.

We vacationed in the sunny south every winter for ten days and met a trendy group of friends every Friday at six pm for after-work cocktails. We always talked about the same things: what southern destination was planned for February, where we were going to ski in March, what kind of car we were planning to lease next year, and occasionally a bit of political banter. We munched on all the latest food trends – not all of which were a big hit I might add. I sneaked roast beef and mashed potatoes into my diet every time my dear husband had to be out for a dental society dinner or guy's night out to do whatever guys do when they're out together. I don't even want to know.

All of this was supposed to make me happy. In fact, it seemed to make all of my friends happy, but I suppose that they thought I was as happy as they were. All of which leads to the obvious question: Was anyone really happy? The fact is that it did not make me happy. Where did I go wrong?

The realization that something in my life was seriously out of synch, or that I was out of synch with my lifestyle, did not come upon me suddenly. It came slowly and insidiously, like a cancer cell slowly and purposefully invading an unsuspecting body. During this cancerous invasion I became acutely aware of two things, both of which led me to recognize that I had a serious problem.

The first thing I considered was that I would not be young forever. Where in the world does that leave Young Urban Professionals? What comes next? I do think that most of my friends did expect to be young forever, and that wrinkles, bags and middle-age spread can come as quite a shock to their narcissistic natures. Then, of course, there would be cosmetic surgeons chomping at the bit to get at another generation.

The second concern, of which I became aware only too clearly, was that my friends were aging before my eyes, and yet they didn't seem to be growing up. The fact was that some of them were aging more rapidly than others. Yuppies are somewhat acceptable when they're young, but they were growing into insufferable individuals. Several of them who had children had the most unspeakable children that you could ever imagine.

If I'm going to make a full confession, I'm going to have to take you back about two and a half years to tell you the story of what it is really like to find yourself at odds with the ranks of the twenty-first century Yuppies. It all happened in a single day.

PART 1

"MAY I INTRODUCE..."

"I have to live for others and not myself; that's middle class morality."
-George Bernard Shaw, Pygmalion, Act V

ONE

I have had two bad habits for as long as I can remember. I have, however, never tried to break either of them, because as you know, most of us actually like our bad habits. If we didn't, they wouldn't be habits. My first unfortunate habit is that I have been an avid magazine collector for as long as I can remember. I subscribe to no fewer than seventeen monthlies, four weeklies and two that come out only twice a year. And these are all paper subscriptions – not even electronic versions. Why I continue to subscribe to the *New Yorker* baffles even me, but some of my friends have noticed them sitting (read: piled) on my coffee table, and have commented on what an erudite magazine it is. In fact, Eric (did I mention that my ex-husband's name is Eric?) insists on having the outdated copies for his waiting room. I have often wondered exactly how many of his dental patients are truly interested in getting engrossed in a *New Yorker* story as they await his ministrations in their mouths. And Eric was the reason I subscribed to *Architectural Digest* and *The Robb Report*. Those, as you may know, are seriously expensive magazines. Whatever. I'm so far behind in my reading, I may never catch up. But I do like a heavy glossy in my hand while sipping a chilled glass of French Chablis late on a Saturday afternoon. Oh dear, maybe I'm not failing at the Yuppie stuff as much as I thought.

The other nasty habit that I particular enjoy is hanging around book stores – big box book stores – in an attempt to determine first whether or not any living soul actually still buys hard copies of the type of books I write then feels comfortable marching up to the cash register with them. Second, I like to know what sort of individual reads the unbridled erotica that spews so implausibly easily from my clearly over-active imagination. This is my way of telling you that the source of my secret income known only to me and my wealth manager at the bank is the royalties from the erotic fiction that I've been writing since before *50 Shades of Grey* made it mainstream. And it seems that I have a large and very faithful following judging from the size of those royalty deposits in my bank account twice a year.

I do have to admit, though, that I get a kind of artistic thrill whenever I actually eyeball someone holding a copy of one of my seven books. They always seem to me to be the most unassuming people who are moved to live a vicarious sex life through my writing. If these people take a furtive look around while reaching for my book on a shelf, then place the book under their arm with the title cleverly concealed, then sidle up to the cashier

10

hoping that no one will actually notice, I can hardly blame them. I suppose this kind of fiction couldn't have become so popular if it hadn't been for electronic books. With a single tap on the screen the book is magically in your e-reader and no one is the wiser. Once when Eric and I were in Barbados, I actually saw someone on the beach reading one of my early books in paperback. She must have been in her mid-fifties with a beefy husband whose brightly patterned swim trunks hovered dangerously close to being half way down his ample butt. As I looked at him it was, to me at least, a no-brainer why she was living vicariously. And it is for those women I write the books. But I also write them for myself.

The truth is that not a living soul outside of my editor and publisher knows the source of my comfortable extra income. My mother who prides herself in knowing every juicy tidbit about everyone would be mightily surprised – perhaps even mortified – if she knew. In fact, not even my wealth manager knows what kind of books I write; he only knows that they're lucrative and he gets to invest the money, none of which was known to Eric whatsoever, and God knows the only thing more dear to Eric's heart than root canals was money. My editor and publisher who do know the real identity of J.L. Kidston are contractually obligated to keep my secret. I'm not nearly ready to come out of the closet yet.

I didn't really set out to hide the fact that I have a passion for writing, or the fact that I am immensely successful at it. In fact, if I wrote for *National Geographic* I would probably have used my bragging rights at one of those dreary, insincerely jolly Friday afternoon cocktail gatherings. However, my chosen style of writing just didn't seem to fit in with our chosen lifestyle (did I mention that was before *50 Shades of Grey* went mainstream?). I had actually started by writing what I considered to be serious literature. Editors did not share my enthusiasm for my self-proclaimed prowess. So, I began to let my imagination take over. It was a complete surprise to me that my fictitious libido seemed to rule the ensuing creative process. Editors loved it.

After my first book sold so well, I went on to write an even steamier second one, so it just naturally evolved into my little secret. Keeping secrets does have its stresses, as I came to find out, but it certainly seemed worth the effort.

The summer of my discontent really began on June 21, 2011 which just happened to be the occasion of my tenth wedding anniversary. Eric and I had been married ten long years. I awoke to a beautiful first day of summer with a gargantuan headache. One might have thought that it was the result of a hangover, which is possibly true, but my hangovers are quite unlike those suffered by most normal people with normal lives. I get them not the morning after a night out, but the morning *before* an anticipated night out. The source of this morning's pain was no mystery this time. It was obviously in anticipation of the anniversary party that our friends, Rebecca and David Rubenstein had insisted on hosting for us that evening. I wondered how I'd ever get through it – the same people having the same conversations about the same things. I started to feel nauseous.

The first sound I heard that morning was the same sound I heard every morning for the past ten years. I was serenaded by the long-familiar strains of Eric gargling in the adjoining master bathroom. From where I propped myself up on the pillows I could just glimpse him ceremoniously measuring his dental floss from the end of his nose to where his arm was held out in front of him at precisely a sixty degree angle. I have never been sure he realized it, but he went through this little ritual every single morning, even on camping trips (although to be fair we had done that only once in our married lives since Eric cannot cope without his requisite twice-daily showers). This procedure irritated me beyond words. I'm not sure why, but it was just one of those things that pushed my buttons.

It was something that as a loving spouse should not have bothered me a bit, but somehow it was a continual vexation. After measuring the floss, he carefully worked at each tooth in succession, moving from one quadrant to the next, looking at the floss between each sweep presumably to determine the effectiveness of his technique. I found the whole process utterly revolting. However, it was a bit like an accident that is so riveting you can't look away ad I had long since given up asking him to close the bathroom door. He complained that this would only contribute to the fogging of the bathroom mirror and to the possibility of mould growth on the walls. Yes, it was an old house, but hadn't we spent a fortune renovating the bathrooms?

"Alex if you don't soon get out of that bed you're going to be late. And I can't smell the coffee. Did you forget to turn it to automatic before you went to bed?" Eric preferred bellowing from the other room to speaking in a modulated tone in the morning. I believe that washing his hair clogged his ears.

"Happy anniversary," I said from underneath the pillows where I had buried my head, and then sotto voce, "Why can't we just get a Nespresso machine like all our friends? And anyway why is it my job?" Yes, I know. The Nespresso thing really is a Yuppie affectation, but the convenience!

14

"What was that?" Eric stuck his head out of the bathroom. "For God's sake get out of that bed, Alex! We have a very busy day ahead of us. I need you to get through that list of errands I prepped for you."

I should have known that this was the project he'd been engaged in before he turned off his iPad the night before. He always seemed to have a very important project to do in bed – and it never included me, it has to be said.

I got out from under the pillow, put on my glasses – I'm as blind as a bat without some sort of visual correction – and picked up my own iPad from under the four magazines on my bedside table. I tapped the mail icon and magically there appeared twenty messages. The first one, with its priority notation, was from Eric. It was his list for me. I had to admit that Eric was, if nothing else, very well organized.

"Why can't you do some of these things," I said when I had my wits about me.

"For God's sake, Alex, don't pout like that. You're too old."

Who was he? My father? Eric was now fastidiously applying short bursts of hair spray to his thinning pate as he spoke. "You know I have a very busy appointment schedule as usual. Mrs. Goldfarb's root canal isn't going to do itself. And you know what she's like. She'll be in the chair most of the morning. I'll just have to charge her for the extra time. You have no idea what it's like to listen to her complaining while she has her mouth open. And then I have that Chamber of Commerce luncheon. I'm speaking as you might well remember."

I sighed and contemplated burrowing back down into the pillows. And why precisely did he think I had nothing to do today? As I watched Eric place every hair in its pre-determined place, I wondered how anyone got psyched up to do a root canal, regardless of the patient's idiosyncrasies. I wondered if he got some sort of sadistic pleasure out of seeing a patient writhing with fear in his waiting room knowing full well the reality of the experience would be every bit as bad as imagined.

Eric was now standing inside his walk-in closet. I could see in the mirror reflecting from my own closet doors that he was peeling off his paisley pajamas. He used to sleep *sans* PJ's, but somewhere along the way his mother had given him those hideous multi-colored monstrosities in multiples, and he had felt compelled to wear them. Mother evidently knows best. No wonder we didn't have any children after ten years of marriage.

As he stood there with his backside to the mirror, I could feel a literary passage coming on. I am well aware that most people do not consider my

16

writing to be literary, but they do read it, so there's something to be said for my contribution to literacy at least. I picked up my iPad and started tapping.

Olivia watched as he ritualistically slid out of his clothes, his burning dark eyes never leaving her face. She had so longed for this moment – she couldn't remember a time when she had not. Trembling with expectation, she closed her eyes momentarily to imagine what lay ahead, but she could not. She opened them to see him standing above her stark naked. She seemed to be his to control – her eyes, her hands, her mouth. She felt more than ready – she had been ready for so very long. He took a step toward her...

"Alex, I asked you a question."

"Sorry, I must have been daydreaming," I said as I slipped the iPad under the covers.

"I've been meaning to speak to you about that," he said clicking his Rolex onto his wrist. "It's becoming quite a problem lately, you know. Last Saturday night at Walter's cocktail party you daydreamed through several conversations. If you want my opinion," (I didn't), "you'll make an appointment to see Walter professionally. You and he could have a nice, useful chat."

Walter was Walter Evans, M.D., F.R.C.P. (C), psychiatrist. Now I was beginning to think that Eric was the one who had lost a few noodles. Walter was just about the most clinically unstable person I had ever met. Nice enough, but seriously weird. Not exactly someone with whom you would share your innermost secrets – at least I wasn't going to.

Eric was now dressed in his immaculate light blue clinic jacket with navy blue trousers. The crease in the trousers was knifelike and precise. I decided that since I had a client meeting at 9:30 all the way in the opposite end of town from my office, I should probably hit the shower myself. Eric always started his office hours at precisely 7:15 am to see all of those patients who couldn't possibly take an hour off from their busy work days to see their dentist. Like most of our friends, they even had their toothaches by appointment. I personally could think of no worse way to start my day than with a dental appointment. Eric never did repeat his question to me; perhaps it just wasn't that important, or he forgot. I watched as he picked up his brief case which contained his iPad and his high-protein granola bar (what else would a dentist carry in a briefcase?). He then pushed his glasses up onto the bridge of his nose and flew down the stairs to his waiting black BMW *ActiveHybrid 5* with all-leather interior. I stepped under the scalding water in the rain shower and wondered how I'd ever survive the party tonight.

TWO

It never occurred to me that after such an inauspicious beginning my day would be anything other than another dull June 21, only to be followed in slow succession by another 365 dull days. How wrong we can sometimes be!

I took two Tylenol #3's to take away the migraine that was threatening to ruin at least my morning if not my entire day, had a cup of black coffee (instant), grabbed my tote bag and headed out the door to my little – and old by Yuppie standards – blue Toyota 4Runner. That car was the real love of my life. Boxy and uncomfortable by European–car-snob standards though it might have been, it had always come through for me regardless of how bad the circumstances: rain, snow, sleet. It had never let me down. That is more than can be said for Eric's Beemer. It was a very good thing it had some kind of special warranty and road-side assistance or we would surely have been in the poorhouse by now. It seemed to spend more time in the service garage than my friend Isobel spent at the spa where she had a frequent flyer card.

I took my usual route to the office, but something felt different this morning. Maybe it was me. I knew that it was really only a difference in my mind, but that's real enough for me. I actually began noticing things that seemed to have slipped right by me in days past. You know, all those little details that you never really see because you're preoccupied with something else, something that always seems to keep you out of the present moment. First I noticed that many people outside our neighborhood took great pride in their properties. In our 'hood it was a given: if you didn't take good care, someone was sure to complain either to you directly or indirectly through someone else who would mention that they had noted a dandelion on your little patch of lawn and weren't you aware that the moment it went to seed the neighborhood would be contaminated? But I was now noticing that it didn't seem to matter that the neighborhood was a bit more down market; the properties looked nice. Here and there I could see residents outside early on this sunny day working in their gardens, raking, pulling weeds, planting pretty, pink annuals whose names eluded me. And they seemed to be enjoying it. Oh to do something just for the pure enjoyment of it!

I sighed, realizing that gardening was more of a competition for our friends. And those of them who had given birth and moved to larger properties had gardeners. When was the last time anyone in our circle ever did anything just because they enjoyed it? Even going to a new pizza place was because the place was trendy and it had to be experienced so you could then ask everyone else if they'd been there yet and relish the thought that you were there first. Dear God, we had spent an hour in a line-up on Ossington Street the previous Saturday night with four friends waiting for a table at a miniscule pizza restaurant because it was the new 'in' place to be. By the time there was a table for us (no reservations permitted), I was so famished I would have eaten the table cloth – if there had been one. We then sat on wooden benches with other idiots who had waited just as long to wait another half hour for our pizza so that it could be lovingly rolled out and baked in the excruciatingly expensive brick oven reportedly brought over from Italy at great expense. Of course the bulk of it was passed on to unsuspecting patrons who endured not only the wait for a table, but whose wallets groaned under the exorbitant price that they were able to command. Was the pizza any good, you appropriately ask? I've had better. The bottom line is that it wasn't nearly worth what we had to go through to experience it, and yet Eric and the other couple we were with waxed on rapturously to other friends who later met us for night caps at another excruciatingly hip cocktail joint – one with retro-country décor that made me gag. But it was hip.

By the time I pulled into the parking garage under my building downtown I was in a foul mood.

I made my way through the layers of security that finally permitted me onto the twenty-seventh floor to the offices of Landers-Pearson Creative, my employer for the past seven years. I smiled tightly and nodded hello to the new receptionist. Where in the world did Lars Pearson find these girls? They were straight off television sit-com offices as far as I could see. They always had perfect teeth, plastic smiles and bags of hammers for brains. They never seemed to last long, though. Where they went after this job was a mystery to me – a mystery that I had neither the time nor the inclination to solve.

As I opened the door to my office I glanced briefly at the name plate on my door: *Alexis Harvey, Senior Account Director*. Before I joined Landers-Pearson I had been working as the communications director for a small museum. I loved the work, but Eric coaxed me to "move up in the food chain" as he used to say. Landers-Pearson will hire you, he had said. What he really meant was that I should demand to be remunerated better for my work. So, I pursued the account manager position here at LP where our stock-in-trade is public relations and marketing, and had been promoted twice since. It was a bit of a natural fit for me, and I liked my job, but rarely experienced the same kind of satisfaction I'd found daily in my non-profit position. I did, however, enjoy seeing the direct deposit in my bank account every two weeks without fail and without fear of someone not making payroll. Although it has to be said that the recent recession did give all of us pause to consider what might happen. We'd been the lucky ones.

I took my cell phone out of my bag and tossed it on the desk where it hit a small package. Hmm, I thought, I wonder who remembered that it was my anniversary. Surely Eric hadn't sent something along?

The small package was wrapped in cheery pink paper and tied up with a silver ribbon. It sat proudly on top of a pile of red file folders that my assistant Pam had no doubt put there the moment she walked in this morning. Maybe she and my colleagues had left it? I didn't think anyone knew about the date – I certainly hadn't told anyone.

My curiosity was quickly alleviated as I ripped open the accompanying card. I should have known: it was from Isobel who had been and continues to be my best friend in the entire world, spa obsession notwithstanding. Isobel, however, was a lawyer in a legal aid office half way across the city, and had never been known as an early riser – unless you count those mornings when she is emerging from an evening-through-morning date and had to get home to shower and change before hitting the office. It had to have been delivered by someone else! In any case I was inordinately grateful that
24

this single-forever (or so she said) friend had sent this little anniversary remembrance to a very grateful friend.

The card read as follows:

Here's to ten long years with the same man. I warned you when you married Eric that he was no ball of fire, but you've made it to number ten in spite of it all! I thought you might need a little something to spice up your married life. Perhaps you can get a few pointers from someone who clearly leads a more exciting life than the rest of us! Enjoy!

I peeled off the pink ribbons and striped paper to reveal none other than a hard-cover copy of J.L. Kidston's latest novel *Welcome to my Fairy Tale*. As had become my immediate habit upon seeing a previously purchased copy of one of my books, I began to mentally calculate my royalty. I knew that Isobel found this kind of erotic chicklit to be her very favorite form of escapism, and for as many years as I had known her, I had always demurred, saying that it wasn't really for me. If she only knew the truth! Of the seven or so books that I had already written, *Fairy Tale* was by far the most fun. I had allowed myself to explore an otherworldly romp and it was great exercise for my imagination.

More than once over the past ten years she had told me how much she enjoyed J.L.'s books. She often opined that this writer must have quite a hot sex life and wondered why she was so mysterious. I once asked Isobel why she thought J.L. was a woman. She just looked at me as if I had two heads. She contended that this J.L. clearly had first-hand experience of the activities about which she wrote. To this I would mentally respond, *never*, my dearest friend, *underestimate the power of the creative mind.* But I had never yet actually said those words to her. Not yet, anyway.

I looked down at the book and started to laugh. I couldn't seem to stop. I sat down at my desk and looked out the window to the high-rise across the street. I was wiping tears of laughter from my face when Pam, my petite assistant with the large glasses and array of twin sets, peeked around the door.

"Everything okay, Alex?" she asked hesitantly.

I cannot imagine what I must have sounded like to her sitting out there in her cubicle. "Oh, yes, Pam. Everything is just fine."

She hesitantly approached the desk and looked at the paper and ribbon now cluttering up my otherwise tidy work area. Then she noticed the book and I could feel an almost physical recoil. Pam was a born-again Christian, although I never could figure out what that had to do with one's consumption of erotica. I could see her face redden

26

ever so slightly. Her eyes widening, she actually began to slowly back away from the desk.

"Oh," she said, "I didn't know you liked that sort of thing." She clutched at her neck where the proverbial pearls might have been.

"This?" I said holding the book up to her.

The face began to redden ever further. She nodded.

"You know this book?"

Her eyes were like saucers now and I knew I had caught my little assistant in whose presence I always made sure not to even swear. I was starting to enjoy this when I realized that she did, indeed, seem to be familiar with this writer.

"Have you read this one?"

She shook her head violently.

"Have you read other J.L. Kidston books?"

She bit her bottom lip and pulled her pale blue cardigan even more tightly around her. I smiled.

"So you have…but just not this one." I held the book out to her. "Well, Pam, it's your lucky day. This is for you."

I'm not sure what kind of a reaction I expected I was going to get. What I didn't expect was that she would actually grab it from my hand, smile slyly and retreat quickly. But she did. So, I thought, old J.L. is contributing to the enhancement of little Pam's life. Good on her!

She hesitated for a moment at the door. "I suppose you don't read this sort of thing."

"Actually," I said carefully, "I've already read it."

She turned back to me and I could see that she seemed to want to say something.

"Something else on your mind, Pam?"

She stopped and took a step back toward my desk. "Can I talk to you, Alex?"

"Of course. Sit down." I came out from behind my desk, closed the door and took the seat beside her. "Are you okay?"

"Umm...not really. It's just that..." A tear emerged from her eye and trickled down her cheek.

I'd never seen Pam so emotional before. Clear-headed, she always seemed to keep the rest of the flighty younger women, interns included, grounded. I was starting to worry. I handed her a tissue from the box on my desk. "You can tell me what's wrong."

"Alex, I feel so stupid. I mean, who else does this happen to these days? And just when I was planning to go back to school this fall." She buried her face in her hands. "I'm pregnant."

I didn't even know she had a boyfriend. "What does your boyfriend think?"

She started to cry.

"You haven't told him, have you?"

"It's complicated," she said. "I can't tell him."

"Why not? He has a right to know. "

"He's married!" She blurted. She was really crying now.

I wasn't sure how to handle this crisis. Pam had always been so sensible, solid, grounded. We sat together for a while until she decided that she'd have to think a bit more about her situation before doing anything. I offered to be there if she needed me. I felt so bad for her.

When Pam left, I turned my attention to the list that Eric had so kindly provided to me early that morning. The first item on the list was, "Pick up dry-cleaning." This was followed by detailed descriptions of every single shirt, trouser and pocket square (don't ask) that I was to retrieve so that I could verify that I, indeed, had gotten Eric's specific laundry, and that I had received every single piece. I could feel my jaw starting to clench and could hear his voice in my ear: "Alex, you really must stop doing that. You know it can cause jaw problems." I sighed. Eric had a phobia of the drycleaner losing his clothes. I had to admit – although I'd be loath to say it out loud to some of our Yuppie friends who were so focused on their 'stuff' – but I have never actually been that attached to anything material. But ten years ago, I had tried to join their ranks.

~

June 21, 2001 had been an especially beautiful Thursday, at least weather-wise. Why would we have a wedding on a Thursday when everyone was supposed to be working? It was summer solstice, a day that had some kind of deep meaning for me at the time. Now I can't really remember what it was! This glorious first day of summer held the promise of fantastic days – and perhaps even years, ahead. I even wondered briefly if there was any truth to the old saying, "Happy the bride the sun shines on." Promises, promises.

I arrived at the church in the back of a black, stretch limousine with my father an appropriate three minutes prior to the scheduled beginning of the ceremony. That would give me enough time to get out of the car, rearrange my train and tulle veil, take my father's arm and proceed to the vestibule. However, as Dad and I made our way up the stone steps and over the threshold of the church we were greeted rather breathlessly by Steven, Eric's older brother, an actuary by occupation.

"You can't come in," he said, barely catching his breath as if he had just finished a marathon, although the way he tripped over his size thirteen feet that day and every other day I had known him, that was an unlikely scenario.

"What do you mean I can't come in?" I said as my best friend Isobel, my maid of honor, carefully helped my train up over the last step. Why did it

30

even have a train? Oh, I remembered: my mother had insisted. "The wedding is about to start, and in case you hadn't noticed, I'm the leading lady in this production."

"Is Eric here?" Leave it to Dad to get right to the heart of the matter.

Steven looked puzzled. "Yes. Why would you ask?"

"Well," Dad said as he straightened his bow tie and uncomfortably adjusted the rented tuxedo, "usually when a member of the groom's family tells a bride she's not welcome in the church..."

"Oh, no," he said, shaking his head, "Eric's here, but Mom and Dad aren't."

I might have known. Eric's parents had never appeared on time for anything in their lives as far as I could figure out. My father, a rather fastidiously punctual sort himself, cleared his throat very loudly, removed a handkerchief from somewhere in the depths of his trouser pocket and wiped his brow. The temperature was rising quickly.

"Where the hell are they?" I hissed.

My father seemed a bit startled at such a response from his daughter in her virginal white wedding dress.

"How am I supposed to know? The fact is they're not here yet and we can't start without them."

I was beginning to wonder unkindly if Steven knew who was paying for this celebration. It certainly wasn't his family.

"Can't you call them and find out? Where's your cell phone? I don't seem to have one on me in this dress!" I said rather unnecessarily sarcastically.

"I left it at home. I didn't want to disturb the ceremony, you know."

"Doesn't anyone else have a cell phone?" I could feel myself getting overheated in this pile of smothering lace.

Steven was standing his ground, now. It was clear I wasn't getting into the church until his parents arrived. I picked up my billowing skirt and made my way back down the steps and back into the limo. As I got into the air-conditioned interior I was thinking it reminded me of a funeral.

Sinking back into the leather seat, I could see a Lincoln Town Car pull into the circular drive in front of the church. It was my soon-to-be in-laws. In what appeared to me to be a very leisurely pace, they disembarked, fixed their collective hair, and slowly made their way toward the steps and up to the door where Steven waited beaming in their direction. They appeared completely oblivious to the fact that they were holding up the ceremony. Dad was now tapping his fingers on the upholstery beside me and checking his watch. He snorted.

"Fifteen minutes late," he said. "Fifteen minutes. What will people think?"

As soon as they cleared the door, I was out of that limo in a flash so that my father had to move quickly to keep up with me. I made it up the steps and down the aisle in record time and we managed to get through the rest of the ceremony without mishap. It wasn't until we were out on the grounds posing for the photographer before heading to the hotel for the reception that I noticed Kevin, Eric's other brother, was wearing brown shoes with his tuxedo. Brown shoes! They stood out like neon signs against the black of his formal trousers. They weren't even clean!

I rather liked Kevin who worked in a lab doing unmentionable things to unsuspecting white rats, but he was as lame-brained as they come, and his wife Sylvia was worse on the social graces score. I wasn't terribly put-off by this little *faux pas*, but my mother who sleeps with a copy of Emily Post under her pillow did take note.

I watched her march right over to poor old Kevin and demand to know if he owned a pair of black shoes.

"Well...yes, I do, actually," he stammered, clearly without the slightest notion of the reason for her enquiry.

"Then where are they?" she said. My mother could be quite intimidating at times.

"I…I think I left them in the office. Why?" He was still in a fog.

I noticed that Sylvia had now inched closer to see what Mom was saying to her husband.

"You are wearing a black tuxedo, young man. When one states black tie, one does not usually feel the necessity to specify black shoes as well!"

He looked down at the offending shoes. I started to snicker behind my bouquet, deciding against intervening. I marvelled at the fact that good old Kevin was nothing like his brother Eric in the deportment department. I wondered if Eric had noticed the aberrant shoes. One thing was certain, though; the shoes would be especially conspicuous in the group wedding photos. I thought it added a nice, funny touch to the whole pompous proceeding, but I knew my mother would be right over to the photographer demanding that they be photo-shopped. It's funny how important events can simply be photo-shopped to appear to be something they weren't. *Sigh.*

Just as at all other weddings, the next fun activity on the agenda was the receiving line. My mother had insisted on it. In her view it was the only way we could be assured of actually speaking to everyone at the wedding. In my view there were far too many people there – a number of whose identities I had absolutely no idea about, and those were guests on the bride's side! I have yet to meet anyone who either likes to be in a receiving line, or even more to the point, likes to have to proceed through one, with the possible exception of my mother, although I think she tended to view it as an obligatory evil.

I suffered through kisses laced with cigar smoke and too much wine from several uncles – had we started serving wine already? Then there was the halitosis rampant among my mother's crowd, the hugs from aunts I couldn't remember, and I'm not a 'huggy' type. Oh, and there were even French kiss attempts from two of Eric's classmates, tongue and all. What in the world were they thinking? To make matters worse, I didn't even remember ever meeting them before.

The receiving line over, we took our places at the head table and before I even had a chance to finish my first glass of wine, it was time for the toast to the bride. I can't now remember how the decision to have Steven deliver this important speech was made or by whom, but there he was, rising from his chair when prompted to do so by the Master of Ceremonies, Kevin.

He rose, clearing his throat several times and calling for the attention of the assembled masses. At that precise moment, someone bumped into

Eric's right elbow which at that very moment attached as it was to his right hand was holding a glass of red wine. Said red wine glass was poised over my white wedding dress, and you know what happened next.

"You're responsible for all future dry-cleaning bills," I said *sotto voce* as waiters ran around with glasses of club soda madly trying to remove the stain that was threatening to take over the entire billowing mass of tulle. There was much mopping up with wedding napkins embossed with our names and general horror at the stain. It crossed my mind in the melee that the dress had cost about $3000 (expensive for 2001), and it had now been worn for a total of one and a half hours. A bit of quick mental math told me that if I changed now, the dress would have cost me $33 a minute. Oh well, you only get married once – I hoped. Then I pasted my smile back on my face and waved to everyone that everything was fine. It most assuredly was not. Indeed, I was beginning to feel a bit of panic set in.

The stain removal process did not go well. The glass had been full and it had landed on the lower part of the tight bodice and leaked down the skirt, soaking all the way through the lining and growing by the nanosecond. There was no question about it – I would have to change. So the toast was postponed for twenty minutes as I retreated to my hotel room to find something else to wear for the

36

rest of the reception. My mother was just about in panic mode now as she accompanied me up in the elevator all the while moaning that the rest of the photos would be ruined.

We managed to find a dress that I had worn the evening before and dolled it up with some new jewelry, returning to the ballroom only to find the nieces and nephews who had not actually been invited to the wedding doing what children do when they are cooped up and bored. They were chasing one another round and throwing hors d'oeuvres at anyone who got in their way. In his booming voice, my father demanded quiet, and he got it.

The toast to the bride, when it finally occurred, was nothing short of embarrassing. Steven had concocted a litany of every girl Eric had ever dated, concentrating particularly on the piece of fluff he had been dating when he met me. I found this to be a rather unusual thematic selection for a wedding toast, and perhaps even a bit tasteless. But it did elicit a few snickers and even a few loud snorts from several of Eric's dental school classmates that made me wonder about his past. Mercifully, however, Eric hadn't really had all that many previous girlfriends, so the list was shorter than it might otherwise have been. Everyone then raised their glass and toasted the bride. I think I detected a few looks of sympathy from several of the women close to the head table. My face was becoming numb with the plastic smile that was pasted there for public view.

Finally, the whole thing was over. We beat a retreat to the airport and jetted off to Nassau in the Bahamas where I spent the next week nursing Eric's sunburn and diarrhea (I just gave him his pills for the latter), and wondering how I had gotten myself into this mess. There were a few funny moments, though.

One morning about four days into the honeymoon, Eric called from the bathroom. "Alex, that's awfully weak mouthwash. And it's too salty. I hope it's not the brand you usually buy."

Puzzled at this remark since I had not brought mouthwash which I in fact never used, I said, "What mouthwash are you talking about?"

"This one," he said waving a bottle of contact lens solution. He didn't have his glasses on.

I started to laugh uncontrollably. By the time I recovered, Eric was ready to string me up since he still didn't see what was so funny. A week before the wedding when I asked my mother if she had a small plastic bottle she gave me a mouthwash bottle and I had put some solution in it. Eric never really forgave me for that mouthwash joke. Pity about his sense of humor.

~

The jangling of the telephone on my desk rudely intruded on my reverie, bringing me abruptly back to the present. It was Isobel.

"Did you get my little anniversary gift?"

"Yes, and thank-you very much," I said. "Have you read it?"

"Is the Pope Catholic? Of course I've read it! Is there a J. L. Kidston book I haven't read? You know me, Alex; I make no apologies for my reading selections. I think I'm possibly the only lawyer in town who usually has one in her briefcase."

More than anything for me Isobel was a breath of fresh air in my often stultified life. During the ten years of my marriage to Eric she had become my one lifeline to reality it seemed. She kept me grounded and connected to the things that more and more I realized really mattered in life. We had spent many a long winter evening in front of the fireplace in her charming little flat discussing the flotsam and jetsam of humankind that populated her legal practice. When she had opted for a legal aid position with its uncomfortable and slightly dingy office in a somewhat shabby, repurposed building, rather than a posh, modern, well-lit corner office in a downtown high-rise, she cut off most of her ties to what had previously been just as much her Yuppie lifestyle as mine. She had married in her second year at law school and by the time she graduated, they had gone their separate ways. I seem to remember her referring to the split as being based on a serious lack of shared values. Her husband was a plastic surgeon who Isobel thought would do volunteer work in Africa fixing cleft lips and palates for indigent children to change their lives. Instead, he had opted for a sub-specialty in cosmetic surgery and now ran a spa/clinic combination where he did face-lifts on women who had more money than brains as far as Isobel was concerned. But she had landed squarely on her feet and was the happiest person I knew.

When she had shown me the advertisement for the legal aid position now some years ago, I remember thinking that she was such a good fit.

"WANTED: Recent law school grad. Must be hard-working, good-natured, desirous of extremely hard work for extremely low pay, lots of job satisfaction for incredibly long hours. Absolute requirement: a good sense of humor."

If there was one thing that Isobel had it was a terrific sense of humor along with her penchant for hard work. She had gone for it and never looked back. I knew, however, that she had now reached that inevitable point of re-evaluation of her career direction – the point we all reach at one time or another no matter how happy we are. This coincided with her need to re-evaluate her personal life, a situation we had discussed only recently.
40

This being said, she had fewer regrets than anyone else I knew, although they would never admit it in the social circles where I travelled these days. I sincerely hoped that she'd find someone, get married and have children someday soon. Isobel, of all the women I knew, would make the best mom ever.

"Are you looking forward to your party tonight?" she said, rather facetiously, I thought.

"Oh, you know me. I can't think of anything I'd rather be doing this evening," I said, just as facetiously. "Except, of course perhaps sticking myself with needles."

Despite the fact that Isobel generally refused to socialize with the crowd that Eric preferred, Rebecca Rubenstein was the hostess of the gathering planned in our honor for that evening; Rebecca happened to be Isobel's cousin, so she was planning to attend.

"Tennis tomorrow afternoon? We can do a party debrief."

"Love to. But why don't we have a drink before the party? Our usual spot?" After Isobel agreed to meet me at our favorite bistro I logged into my secret files in the cloud and started typing.

Olivia sat in the stands with the rest of the steaming masses. She could think of nothing else

41

now but the night they had spent together. To now watch him in the light of day, every muscle straining against his shorts as he expertly returned each serve from his opponent she could yet feel the thrust of his body against hers. She breathed deeply and focused her attention on the game at hand. Just then she noticed his opponent. He was just slightly taller, just slightly more chiseled. As the game ended, he seemed to glance up at the stands. Did he catch her eye for a moment or was she dreaming? I must have him next, she said. Tonight. Olivia slid out of the stands to make her plans...

THREE

In the vernacular of the past few decades, Eric and I were classic D.I.N.K.'s (you know, double income, no kids). The label itself connotes so many idiosyncrasies of a relationship that just happened to be true for the two of us. We had a very good cash flow, sizable equity, lots of freedom to do exactly what we desired, and no one to answer to but ourselves. What all of this resulted in was that we were probably two of the most self-centered people you could ever know – but we weren't alone. All of our so-called friends (with the exception of Isobel) were just like us. It seems to go with the territory.

I was sitting at my desk later on that afternoon of my anniversary contemplating this rather depressing fact when I happened to check the time on the bottom right-hand corner of my computer screen. It was much later than I thought. And I had much to do if I was going to accomplish all those little tasks so thoughtfully set out for me by my dear husband. I had already picked up his laundry on my quick run out for a yogurt and berries at lunch time, noting with some confusion that it seemed to include a sweater I'd never seen before. The next item on the list was: "Pick up two bottles of Moët & Chandon champagne." He had to be that specific because he knew that left to my own devices I'd have picked up Veuve Clicquot. Veuve was my favorite, but Eric preferred the Moët. I thought I'd probably split the difference once I got to the liquor store.

As I wandered past Pam's desk on the way out, I noticed the copy of *Welcome to My Fairy Tale* peeking out from under a sheaf of papers beside the blotter. I noticed a book mark sticking in it – it looked to me as if she had already read a fair amount. Must have been a hot and heavy lunch hour, I thought, smiling. I turned around and bumped right into her as she rounded the corner, likely from the ladies room.

"Oh, Alex, I'm so sorry." Pam looked toward where the book was protruding from the papers reddening slightly.

"See you tomorrow?" I said, ignoring her discomfiture. "And don't worry. Everything will turn out okay."

She nodded and sidled toward her desk, moving the papers so that the book was covered completely. I was still smiling when I punched the elevator button. But by the time I'd arrived in the building lobby, the warm feeling was gone. I had the evening's festivities to face – and there was still the rest of the damn list.

The day was oppressively hot with everyone moving in slow motion. I joined the throng of tourists in their gigantic white sneakers and fanny packs, finding myself becoming a part of the torpid movement. The humidity surrounded me like cotton batting.

As I reached the liquor store, I fumbled around in my shoulder bag pulling out a five dollar bill to put into the can held by that unfortunate man who sits in front of every liquor store in the country – or so it seems. You know the one, always there with his hand out. I always felt sorry for him, but whenever I reached for my wallet, Eric never ceased to point out that we have a very extensive system of social services in our country and that the man sitting there might even make as much money as I did. I was never certain what he really meant by that: was it a jab at the fact that I made less money than he did? Or was he just an insensitive boor that I was beginning to resent? Anyway, Eric wasn't with me and it was my anniversary. My present to myself was to give that man the five dollars and see the smile on his face. I was not disappointed – and for once I didn't care if he used it for something less than healthy.

I opened the door of the liquor store and was hit with a blast of air conditioning. I savored it for a moment and headed straight for the champagne/sparkling wine shelves, immediately feeling an overwhelming sense of mischief. My hand lingered for only a moment over the bottle of Veuve and then before you could say Baby Duck, one of the Ducks was in my cart. Then it struck me: just last weekend we had toasted our next door neighbor's new car (who does that sort of thing?) with a couple of bottles of Moët. That meant that two empties were now sitting in my blue box awaiting recycling pick-up. I looked over at the shelf of cheap sparkling wines and picked up two of the cheapest off the shelves. I would transfer them to the Moet bottles and re-cork them as best I could. I would only have to be assured that no one but me had a chance to see them or open them. I could pull it off and Eric would pretend to love it.

Just as I was relishing the thought of my prank, I spotted Robert LaChance contemplating the French Bordeaux. Robert was one of Isobel's law school classmates, and the only way to describe him is to say that he is a smarmy conglomeration of every unpleasant trait known to be displayed by the male of the species. Others might see him as a charming Frenchman, looking several years younger than his thirty-five years, and possessing a distinct resemblance to Leonardo DiCaprio. I just found him disgusting.

He was deep in conversation with someone I didn't recognize. The other man was not wearing the lawyer-like uniform that Robert and his colleagues sported. There was no expensive suit and tie, no Italian leather shoes, no Prada tie. His dark hair, streaked interestingly with silver, fell over his collar at the back, and he was wearing dark jeans and a tweed jacket with leather elbow pads – an odd choice for such a hot day, in my view. He looked fascinating. He didn't look at all like the sort Robert cavorted with.

I was trying not to eavesdrop, but I couldn't help but catch a few snippets of their conversation as I examined the bottles of port, trying to avoid an actual encounter with the disagreeable Robert. I gathered that this man was quite familiar with Robert, and as far as I could make out, he was some sort of accountant judging from the numbers they were throwing around with words like "capital" and "compounded." Suddenly their conversation seemed to be over, ending abruptly and angrily, or so it seemed to me. Robert had not yet noticed me.

I went about my business, keeping my head lowered slightly, hoping that I could avoid detection, and that Robert would simply buy his Bordeaux and leave. As I concentrated on the Madeira, I felt a pat on my back side. I turned quickly only to find Robert with a sleazy grin on his face.

"Robert LaChance, do that again and I'll slap your face."

He smiled widely, flashing a set of teeth straight out of Hollywood, or his dentist's office – I happened to know that it was the latter. He grinned impishly, flashing his green eyes. If I hadn't known him for as many years as I did, and had not been privy to some sordid stories about his womanizing ways, I might have fallen prey to his good-looking dash. But I knew the real Robert – so I knew better.

"I am so sorry, my darling Alex, but your beautiful bottom, she does so invite the touch, no?"

Somehow the French accent always made the sleazy sound seductive, but I was not to be fooled. Sleaze was sleaze.

"My bottom invites no such thing, and you should know enough to keep your hands to yourself." I picked up a bottle of Madeira and placed it into my cart next to the two bottles of Baby Duck, hoping he hadn't noticed them.

"Alexis, *ma chère*, Renée and I are so looking forward to the soiree in your honor this evening." I think he might have actually winked at me. "Of course, for you *and* your delightful husband."

I'm not sure, but it occurred to me that Robert may just have been the only man to ever wink at me in my entire life – and not in a good way. And he might have been the only person in the world to ever refer to Eric as 'delightful.'

48

"Ten years is a long time to be married to one man, is it not?" he said.

What exactly was he implying? I shuddered.

"Ten years is a long time to be doing just about anything, Robert. How long have you and Renée been married now?"

"We have had now five years of the wedded bliss. But of course, we do the wedded bliss differently."

Did he wink at me again? Wedded bliss, is that what he called it? I had heard rumors – and according to the gossip, Robert was the only party in that relationship who "did wedded bliss differently." But of course no one would ever mention a word to Renée – at least not if one valued one's sanity. Renée had never been known as the most stable person. And her level or Yuppie pretention was exceeded only by her abiding belief in the sanctity of her union with the smarmy Robert.

Robert and I exchanged a few more banalities of the day about the weather. "Well, Alexis, I shall see you and Eric later," he said as he let his hand linger just a nanosecond too long on my forearm.

As I made my way out of the liquor store and back into the wall of heat that hit me in the face, I was feeling even less like attending the party than I had earlier if that was possible. Why in the world had I let Eric talk me into being one half of the guest of honor at this little shindig planned for this evening? When Rebecca had offered to host the party in our honor, Eric had immediately agreed before I had a chance to beg off. I should have been more forceful.

I slid into my car and for once wished that I had air conditioning. I opened up all the windows and let in the dank humidity. I wasn't sure which was worse. As I settled myself behind the wheel, I was remembering a day I had spent with Robert several years earlier, and it had been Robert who had finally saved me from declaring Yuppie failure at that precise moment.

~

It had all started with the searing realization that every Yuppie has to have a sport. And not just any sport will do. Wrangling alligators in a swamp won't cut it. Darts, ping-pong and roller derby are also on the list of unsuitable pursuits for a bona fide Yuppie. Alpine skiing, on the other hand, is at the top of the winter sports choices.

Deprived as my adolescence and early adulthood must have been, I had never learned to ski (cross-country skiing didn't really count). I have tried and failed to figure out the precise criteria that have to be used to determine the suitability of a sport for Yuppies, but my best guess would be that the following axiom is true: The suitability of a sort for a bona fide Yuppie is

50

directly proportional to the amount of money it takes to (a) outfit yourself for said sport; (b) take lessons for said sport; and (c) actually perform said sport. In addition, it must involve a trip to some very expensive location at least once a year after which you must return home to regale all your friends with tales of your adventure and you must continue to do this for six months whenever you can find a fresh ear.

What all this meant to me, or more specifically to Eric and his never-ending quest to make me into a Yuppie, was that I would have to put away any notion of continuing my interest in Nordic skiing and head for the hills. So that is just what I did. Unfortunately, as usual, Eric could not possibly spend a day away from his office to accompany me in this pursuit, but he was adamant that I should go. Robert, hearing of our little dilemma as we discussed it at a cocktail party, could clearly not resist the opportunity to spend an entire husband-sanctioned day with someone else's wife. He could barely contain his enthusiasm. Thus, volunteering to sacrifice himself to the gods of Yuppiedom, and refusing to hear my protestations as to the lack of necessity for this magnanimous offer, Robert became my skiing mentor, god help us all.

My first indication of impending Yuppie failure should have been when I refused to invest a single cent in equipment or clothing prior to my first day on the slopes. And it wasn't that no one tried to get me to make the purchases. I had dutifully accompanied Eric to the 'Ski Shop' in January when the sales started. Everyone had insisted that I would enjoy the experience so much more if I had my own boots. I was at least willing to look.

We entered the 'Ski Shop' to be greeted by what I began to refer to as the "slope folk." With a kind of lululemon fervour, the perky blonde sales associate, accompanied by her hulking blonde sidekick with the chiselled cheekbones, materialized at our side to offer her expertise to our shopping experience. Eric smiled at her and accepted.

She showed us first to the sale racks mainly because I told her in no uncertain terms that I wanted to start there. We spent about twenty minutes perusing the racks – or should I say Eric perused while I eavesdropped on conversations around me, trying all the while to get a feel for the "slope folk." I was fascinated by the jargon and the sales pitches. All of the sales associates seemed to be leading their customers to believe that they themselves were world-class skiers, and the right equipment and clothing could do the same for them. Puhlease!

While Eric carried on a high-level ski conversation with the blonde sales associate, I moved around the racks so that I could better

52

observe one of the other over-muscled sales persons sell a complete ski package to what appeared to be a boy about sixteen years old while his parents looked on with pride.

"Push your ankles toward the front of the boots and bend your knees," he was saying to the young customer. "That's it, bend your knees. Just feel it." With that his eyes fluttered heavenward. I was certainly not sure that "it" was the he was supposed to feel, but I was fascinated that the customer seemed to be able to "feel it" along with the sales associate.

"That feels great," he said.

I thought he was going to take out a cigarette and sit back in bliss. (I could feel an idea forming in the back of my mind and reflexively shoved my hand in my tote bag to root around for my notebook.)

"Gee, I think I'll be able to tackle the black diamond runs at Mount Ste. Anne at March break," the young customer said as he tightened the menacing-looking straps that folded over to close the boots.

Black diamond? I was fairly sure that it was a brand of cheese. I knew that I had bought some only last week at the supermarket. What did cheese have to do with skiing? Perhaps it had another meaning? *That must be it*, I thought, turning back to the action so as not to miss a thing.

The sales associate was now over beside the rack of skis trying to determine which ones to try to sell with the boots. I figured he was likely concerned about safety and the ability of the skier, no? Well, I was wrong.

"If you just slip out of the boots, I'll put them together with the skis and you'll be able to see how good the ones I've chosen look together." He took the gray boot with the blue and red stripes and placed them atop a pair of shiny fire-engine red skis with grey and blue stripes. Then he turned and pulled a red ski suit off the rack behind him.

I stole a surreptitious glance at the price tag, almost swallowing my tongue in the process. In spite of the fact that I had developed great skill the stealthy price check since being married to Eric who thought that price didn't matter if you loved something. (Maybe he should have thought of that and checked with me before he chose my engagement ring...but I digress.). I had to learn this skill simply for survival: I had a nasty visceral reaction to buying anything whose price I did not fully comprehend. But that day, when I caught sight of the prices, I was stunned – or gobsmacked as one of my British friends says. I could not believe that the parents would contemplate paying such a sum for a kid who had not yet finished

54

growing. If it fit him until the end of this ski season, it would be a minor miracle.

"Now you can get the full effect," said the salesman as he proudly displayed his wares.

The group of them – young customer, parents and assorted sales associates who had come to offer a chorus of support – spent the next few minutes admiring the effect and then a few more discussing it. There was evidently no attempt to hurry ski shoppers – but given the individual purchase amount, it was hardly a surprise.

"We'll take the whole thing," Mother was saying as she reached for her platinum American Express card. Father did not appear quite as convinced and I found myself rooting for him. Go Dad, go! He fingered the price tag gingerly, but said nothing. Years of experience, perhaps?

"I'll be back on Tuesday, "said Mother, "to try on some new arrivals myself."

This was finally too much for Father. "What's wrong with the ski suit I bought you last year in Chamonix?"

"Don't be silly, darling," she said as if she were addressing a young, naïve and rather dim-witted child. "It's last year's style." With that she took his arm and he allowed himself to be led away to the cash register. Their son looked very pleased with himself as he brought up the rear.

Now it was our turn.

"Have you made a few selections?" Blondie was saying to me, her ponytail flapping in time to her enthusiasm.

I had not, but I could see that Eric had. He was holding two ski suits: one was white with splashes of magenta down the arms and legs (*The better to see you lying face down in the snow?* I wondered.) The other one was turquoise – couldn't miss me in that one.

"My wife needs a pair of ski boots. She's never skied before, but plans to take lessons this year."

Blondie eyed me again, this time a bit more skeptically. Or was it pity? It was hard to tell with these slope folk. She seemed to be sizing me up.

"I think in that case comfort should be your main concern. Next year you can get a bit more adventurous."

Who was she kidding? Adventurous? And more ski purchases the next year? *Not going to happen*, I thought. *But that comfort idea, it's right on the money.*

She reached for a shoe-sizer while I sat down on the wooden bench.

"That looks to be a size eight," she said as she sent her side-kick who had been hovering on the periphery to find some boots. She mumbled some ski-speak to him and he was back in a flash.

56

He placed the molded-plastic contraptions on the floor in front of me and I slid my feet into the rear-entry (it has to be said that I found the term rather unnerving) models while Blondie's assistant carefully and in my view patronizingly demonstrated how to fasten them. I stood up and promptly fell over. As I lay there sprawled in a very unlady-like fashion on the floor, I could see that I was now the main attraction in the store. And I could see Eric's face begin to redden from the neck up.

"For the love of god, Alex, try to be a little less uncoordinated. This doesn't bode well for the ski lessons."

And that had been precisely what I'd been trying to tell my loving and evidently deaf husband for weeks before this little incident. I was uncoordinated and had dealt with this my entire life. Why did he suppose I had so little interest in playing sports?

"I had no idea that ski boots were so rigid," I said pouting slightly. Rigid...where was that damn notebook? I stood up carefully; or rather I was hauled up by Eric and the assistant's assistant. Finally, I was once again upright.

"Now, bend your knees," Blondie and her assistant said simultaneously, just as the other sales associate had said to his young customer.

So, I bent my knees and nearly fell ass over kettle yet again. I was beginning to feel ridiculous. Strike that. I was beginning to feel even more ridiculous.

"I think these are all right," I said to Eric who was now looking over some equipment for himself pretending not to know me.

Blondie was distraught. "They have to be more than just all right!" She said this with such a passion that I almost believed her. "They have to be perfect!"

"I'm sorry," I said, "but I don't think I'd know what perfect is supposed to feel like if it hit me in the face. Ski boots are new to me." I twisted to see if I could see the price tag without falling on my… well, you know. "How much are they?"

"Cost cannot really play a part when buying comfortable and safe ski equipment, ma'am."

"How much are they?" I repeated, and I hated having to repeat myself.

"These ones normally retail for $450.00 but we have them on for $399.00 today. It's a real steal."

I began to feel faint. "Get me out of these things." I thumped down on the bench and fiddled with the aluminum buckles. "Eric, I can't justify that kind of money for something I'm not sure I'll get very much use out of and that I can rent anyway."

"You won't find rental ones lined with this Polyolefin," said Blondie.

I didn't give a rat's ass at that point about Polyolefin or anything else. I couldn't get the buckles undone, so stood up and took a step toward Eric who was standing off to one side and who might not have heard me. Having never actually walked in ski boots before, I took two steps and fell head first into him. This was definitely too much for him. Needless to say, I headed to my first ski lesson that winter with rented equipment.

I borrowed a ski suit that had seen better days from my brother-in-law Kevin. It was puce green and not really meant for women, but I didn't care. I had my cheap goggles that I'd let Eric buy for me and then stood in line with about a million junior high school students on a school ski trip at the ski rental hut at 8 am on a beautiful February morning. I could not remember ever having gotten up that early when I didn't have to be either at work or at the airport for an early flight. But the early bird gets the ski rentals.

Robert hadn't seemed to care that my attire was less than fashionable that morning when he had picked me up in the cold dark of 6 am. True to his word, he was going to see that I had a ski lesson and a day on the slopes while Eric tended to a few root canals. As the sun came up over the mountain, I scanned the crowds. My non-descript attire seemed to melt into the background as the fashion show began. There was all manner of fashionable ski sits. There was the purple-suited blonde whose skis even matched precisely the tone of the suit. There was the older woman in green and white stripes and silver boots. There were skin-tight one-piece suits, and puffer-style jackets with sleek black ski pants. There were Dolce & Gabbana, Gucci goggles and Prada neck warmers. There were more designer watches than I could count. It never occurred to me to see if any of them could actually ski – it was all about the parade of fashion. Perhaps it didn't really matter anyway.

After I made it through the line with the children, I was ready to gear up for my lesson. Robert – god love his lecherous soul – was right there to tell me which was the right boot and which the left one. This was not clear to me. He showed me how to fasten them so tightly that I thought they would cut off my circulation, and then he showed me how to get into and – more importantly in my view – how to get out of the skis. Robert was uncharacteristically patient. But then it was time for "The Lesson."

FOUR

Robert helped me to shuffle over to the bottom of what they called "the bunny hill." I was just wondering why it was called that if it was really the "kiddie hill" (there seemed to be no one other than little kiddies on it) when a tall, good-looking ski instructor was suddenly at my side. I was to have this Adonis all to myself for an hour after which I was expected to join Robert on what I supposed was a real ski hill. Robert would then capitalize on what I would presumably learn and try to hone my skills just a little. Well, that was the plan, anyway.

Serge was his name. And he had a smile that was all blindingly white teeth. Eric would have been proud – although his hygienist would have had a fit. As far as she was concerned, people were over-whitening. In any event, I supposed that Serge was a Yuppie since this obsession with white teeth was very common among my acquaintances. Serge told me that he would help me to get up the little hill, down the little hill, and how to protect myself from being killed by either myself or one of the assorted tots who were also on the bunny hill, none of whom had either skill or fear. I alone had fear.

Side-stepping my way up the hill was actually easy. I mastered that on the first climb to the top.

61

Coming down using what Serge called the "snow-plough" technique was not so easy. The real terror, though, didn't strike until he told me it was time to tackle the rope-tow.

Rope-tow? What about chair-lifts? According to Serge, chair- lifts came later, much later. The rope-tow looked easy enough I supposed as I looked at it slowly moving children up the hill as they held on with their little mitten-covered hands. It wasn't. It wasn't even close to being easy. Indeed, what happened next might just go down in the history of my life as the most embarrassing things I have ever had the misfortune of doing.

As a result of having a private instructor, I was able to proceed to the front of the straggly line of children who were queued up for the tow. That was very nice, but what it really amounted to was that about a hundred kids watched as I fell up the hill. How does one fall up a hill, you might reasonably wonder. Well, I believe that I just might be the world expert, having practically dislocated my left shoulder. I could feel it lift out of its socket. I had no idea how sore I would be the next day.

"Lift it up! Lift it up!" was all I could hear Serge saying. He was shouting at me from the bottom of the hill as I fell ass over kettle into the snow causing a sizeable pile-up of young bodies behind me. It was like a multi-colored braid with stray strands waving and thrashing in the breeze. It

62

is impossible to fall in the rope-tow line and not cause such a display.

"I think you better get new mittens," Serge said when he arrived at my side to help me up. They had stopped the tow line so that we could all right ourselves and continue to the top, such as it was. Serge was looking at the shiny, slippery palms of the mittens I had worn tobogganing as a kid. They had been the only ones I could find that morning: a detail forgotten in the preparations.

I finally did make it to the top and felt damn proud of myself. But it had been no easy feat. I then turned around and looked down at the gentle grade – I knew intellectually that it was gentle, but as far as I was concerned, it was a precipitous drop-off filled with moguls (or were they just children who had fallen on their way down?). With a bit of a nudge from Serge, or rather a slap on the back, I was able to make it down without too much real difficulty; that is if you don't count the fact that I lost control before I was half-way down, forgetting to use that snow-plough stance, and made my final descent at what felt like 80 miles an hour all the while hoping that those unfortunate people at the bottom of the hill had the sense to look up and get out of the way because I had no earthly idea how to stop. That was in the next lesson.

I don't know how I did it, but at the very last moment before I ploughed into the rope-tow line-up, I managed to turn my skis together (beginner's luck I guess) so that I stopped just short of the children who were now pointing and staring. I managed to stay upright and recoup at least a shred of dignity. The thrill of speed that "real" skiers talk about seemed to have eluded me. Right about that moment, Robert appeared, and I'm certain that I heard a sigh of relief escape Serge's lips.

"How does it go?" Robert said brightly. "I knew that you would be a born skier."

He had clearly not been near the bunny hill during the past hour. Serge rolled his eyes but had the sense to keep his mouth shut. For that I was at least grateful.

Robert and I then spent a half an hour making our way toward the chair lift and I guess he could feel my mounting alarm. Instead he said, "I am a bit cold today, Alex. How does it go with you if we go to the lodge for a bite to eat and perhaps a drink?"

I could have hugged the man at that moment. When at last I had extricated myself from the slats of terror, I was ready for just about anything Robert might offer further. He took my hand and led me into the ski lodge which was the nicest, and it has to be said, safest part of my day despite the copious amounts of beer I then imbibed. Robert also had

64

beer; a situation that he said would be our little secret. In case you don't know, the Yuppie code prohibits the consumption of beer in favor of vintage wines and spirits. The beer, however, went beautifully with the chili that we ate sitting an arm's length away from the very large, stone fire pit that took up the center of the lodge that was itself shaped like a very large tee-pee.

We had a fairly wide-ranging conversation until the beer muddled my thoughts. We talked about our spouses at length – at least Robert talked about his spouse; I don't remember saying very much about Eric since Robert didn't seem to be very interested in him.

I had known Robert and Renée for some years and was under the impression – the one so carefully created by Renée – that they had a marriage just about as close to ideal as one could be. After my conversation with Robert that day, however, his tongue just slightly loosened by the beer as well as distance from his wife, it was crystal clear to me that Robert had something of a wandering eye. And I suspected that his eye was not the only part of his anatomy that was doing the wandering. From that moment on, it was clear that Robert's interest in in me was more (or less?) than platonic. Our relationship was never the same again.

~

Thoughts of the winter cooled me only momentarily. I was still sitting in the car in the parking lot at the liquor store. I shook my head and put the car in gear. As luck would have it, at just that moment, I noticed Renée approaching her Audi which was parked at the farthest edge of the lot. She must have just missed Robert.

She didn't notice me sitting there with the engine running; ordinarily I would have just pulled out of the parking lot before one of those earnest tree-huggers started tapping on my window to tell me that idling is bad for the environment, but there seemed to be something just a bit unusual about Renée's behavior. I decided to sit there for just a moment longer to watch.

She must have gone in and out of the store with lightning speed to have missed both Robert and me, but she had obviously made a purchase because she had a small brown paper bag under her arm. I wondered if she might be ill; her usually impeccably coiffed blonde hair was more tousled than usual, and the trousers she was wearing looked less than pristine, at least from where I sat crouching down as far as I could without impeding my view.

I watched her as she placed her hand on the handle to open her car door; she turned her head both ways, seeming to scan the parking lot (was she looking for Robert?). Now my curiosity was really piqued.

Have you ever had the experience of being so curious about something then, having finally discovered the answer, wished that you had not asked the question? I should have simply backed out of the parking spot when I got in the car because when I saw Renée LaChance, the self-proclaimed epitome of the ideal Yuppie wife sitting in her brand new Audi 8 take a swig out of the bottle in the brown paper bag, I knew that I now had too much information.

She took another then dabbed at her lipstick with the back of her hand. She took another swig then ducked her head, presumably to tuck the open bottle under the driver's seat. She then sat up and started the car, pulling away oblivious to the fact that she had been watched. I felt like a voyeur.

I took a deep breath and wondered how I'd face her at the party tonight. With any luck she'd pass out before the appointed time. I just prayed it wouldn't be behind the wheel of her car.

FIVE

I was preoccupied as I drove home through early rush-hour traffic. In fact, I was so distracted that as I pulled into our street, I almost took the bumper off a white Porsche parked at the curb in front of our neighbor's house. There would have been hell to pay for that for sure! My preoccupation was with Renée and her liquor store parking lot behavior. As much as she got under my skin with her holier-than-thou attitude, always taking the moral high ground on any number of issues, I was bothered – perhaps even concerned. Dare I say worried?

Renée and I had never been the best of friends. In some ways we were – I shudder to even admit it – quite alike. We were both stubborn and opinionated, but I always liked to think that over the years I had learned to get my own opinions under control. I no longer felt the necessity to spout off on all topics. Added on to that was the fact that I'd been noticing that as I got older, it mattered less and less that others should be privy to my opinions. It was enough for me to simply know in my own mind and heart that others were so often wrong, while I was right! Renée on the other hand, still found it necessary to let everyone else know that she was right. And she was always right (at least in her opinion).

Renée Comeau-LaChance was a 40-year-old, newly re-employed social worker (only very part-time of course – remember the children's needs, not to mention Renée's own penchant for tennis and hot yoga which took up hours of every week). I had never quite understood how it came to pass that this seemingly self-absorbed fashion plate got a degree in social work. Although she often spoke of her work before the two children arrived, I had no direct experience of her ever having worked. Sometimes I even thought that she had made the whole thing up. Then, when her youngest was safely in school for many hours a day, in the middle of Friday night cocktails, she announced to everyone that she had procured a new job. We were surprised, to say the least, but the oddest part was that Robert seemed as shocked as the rest of us. Anyway, she worked two afternoons a week in a shelter for homeless youth, and that had given her a new boost up onto the moral high ground, or so it seemed. One other thing that seemed to vex her terribly was that she was three years older than her husband. In my view, she should have been married to someone twenty years older and wiser who might tell her when to button it once in a while. I had noticed that as much as

Robert was a smooth operator, he usually acquiesced to Renée in almost everything. One has to suspect that this approach would keep the peace at home.

Renée's recent return to the workforce was based on her belief that every mother – not just her – ought to stay home for precisely the same amount of time that she did, and then return to work for precisely the number of hours she did so as to divide her time equally among her work, her children, her personal grooming and maintenance, and her husband. At least I think she planned time for her husband, but I didn't really know. Renée could tolerate neither career women who re-entered the workforce with infants at home, nor what she called perpetual housewives who chose to stay home for more than the first few years. And as for her opinion on the whole home-schooling thing that was actually beginning to gain a foothold in the Yuppie culture, she put home-schoolers in the same category as she did people who wore socks in sandals. To say that Renée was dogmatic in her approach to the world would be rather an understatement.

One thing that was especially memorable about Renée was that she loved to give parties. No intimate little, informal dinner parties for her, though. That was my style, much to Eric's consternation. No, Renée's favorite kind of party was the 'theme' party. As a matter of fact, for a few years there, I cannot remember going to a party at anyone's house that wasn't some kind of a theme party. At that time, one had to have a theme or one simply didn't have a party.

~

The first party I ever attended at the LaChance's home was a "Great Gatsby" party. It was a revelation for me who had just recently finished grad school and was used to beer and pretzel parties. Instead, everyone at this party was dressed in white, complete with straw hats and parasols. This was long after Robert Redford had done his turn at Jay Gatsby, and some years before Leo DiCapprio took his turn. Fortunately for me at the time, Eric had known exactly what I should wear to the party, assisting me with all of the pre-party details. I particularly remember that Renée served champagne with drowning strawberries in open coupes rather than flutes, and the salads were all made from vegetables with unpronounceable names, and that was long before vegetables with unpronounceable names were in vogue.

Another of Renée's famous parties had been the 'Tarts & Vicars" party. That one had been a real hoot. All the men were required to arrive decked out in clothes that they supposed might have been worn by old-time clergy. The women, on the

71

other hand, were to dress as street hookers of yesteryear. I remember opening the invitation and immediately responding with, "This has got to be the stupidest idea Renée has come up with yet. I for one won't be going."

Eric was unimpressed with me. "Of course you're going," he said matter-of-factly. Although Eric hated to dress in what he called 'funny clothes,' he was loath to have anyone think he wasn't part of the fun crowd. He wasn't, but that didn't seem to bother him, or he was completely unaware.

He never ceased to amaze me when it came to doing things for the sake of appearances. From time to time I tried to rack my brain to remember if he'd always been like this. How could I have married someone so caught up in appearances? Then, it occurred to me that I used to care more about what other people thought of me, and Eric cared less. Over the past few years, we seemed to have grown in different directions. In any case, on the night of the party, there we were, bundling ourselves into Eric's Beemer looking like two escapees from a B-grade movie from the 1940's.

Eric was fiddling with his parson's collar and I was checking my garters when I looked behind us to see flashing lights. Then the siren started. Eric looked in the rear-view mirror.

"Damn it," he said starting to pull the car over to the curb.

The police cruiser pulled up behind us and I watched as the officer got out and made her way toward the door. Eric opened his window and peered out at the pretty, young police officer.

"Excuse me...Reverend," she said noticing Eric's collar. "But are you aware you ran that stop sign..." Her voice trailed off as she peered further into the car at me.

I looked down at my fishnet stockings and the red satin mini skirt that I was wearing with the black leather bustier. I smacked my lips together – I was unused to wearing such heavy lipstick. (I need to mention that it was the same color as the red satin miniskirt.) I had taken great pains to apply my makeup in what I believed to be the most tartish, whoreish style I knew. Evidently I had succeeded, because the officer was fixated on me.

"Madame, I'm going to have to ask you to get out of the car," she said authoritatively.

I was now beginning to really love this; Eric was clearly mortified.

"Officer, I think I can explain."

"Oh, I'm sure you can, Reverend. I know your type."

"But you don't understand."

"You, out of the car as well," she said to Eric as she beckoned to her partner who was still in the police cruiser.

Her partner responded quickly, opening the passenger door to let me out after I unlocked from the inside. He was her back-up, no doubt, to help her deal with these hardened criminal types. I was starting to get the giggles.

"You don't understand," Eric said again as he gave the officer his license and registration cards. "I'm not a reverend and she's not a…"

"Not a what?" I said. "Whose idea was this, anyway?"

"This isn't funny," Eric said, as I started into a fit of giggles.

I got out of the car and stood there smiling at the male officer. I suppose we looked like hardened criminals – or veritable loonies.

What followed was a lengthy explanation, along with Eric producing his dental license. (Who carries around a wallet-sized dental license, anyway? Is there ever likely to be a dental emergency on an airline flight where they might require you to show your license before administering assistance to the woman with the severe toothache in the back of the plane?)

Finally, it seemed as if we had convinced the two officers that there was no felony being committed. They permitted us to get back into the car and get on our way to the party. As Eric put the car in gear muttering that they at least seemed to have forgotten the reason for pulling him over in the first place, there was a knock on the window.

"Almost forgot, sir," said the woman police officer, tearing a ticket off her pad and handing it in through the window Eric had lowered to hear her.

When we finally arrived at the party a few minutes later, the cop car was still following behind us as if they wanted to ensure that there, indeed, such a peculiar party in a well-regarded neighborhood. We walked up the front steps and rang the doorbell. The door opened to reveal Renée dressed in almost the identical outfit that I was wearing – although it has to be said that it did look better on her. She seemed somehow more the part than I did. When Robert came up behind her, wine glass in hand, the police car drove off. It was the highlight of the evening.

One thing I could never understand in those days was why our crowd of friends and acquaintances could not just have a party where people eat familiar, comfortable food, make their own decisions about what to wear, and generally have a good time. It seemed too much to ask.

One of Renée's other memorable parties was the one heralded by an engraved invitation (who does that these days?) that said the following:

> *The pleasure of your company is requested*
> *for*
> *an alfresco dining experience*
> *Etc.*
>
> *Dress: Casual*
> *R.S.V.P.*

I was a bit nervous about the 'etc.' part. The pretentiousness knew no bounds: the invitation was in reality for a backyard barbeque. My idea of a barbeque was hamburgers and hot dogs on paper plates accompanied by good beer, and maybe a glass or three of red wine from a box. It seemed that my party evolution had been halted at about third year university. In the olden days, the main-course burgers might have been followed by a touch football game or more food, preferably chocolate ice cream and gloppy cake.

Populated as our circle of friends was with vegetarians at the time of Renée's invite (thank god that went out of fashion to be replaced by the gluten-phobic – at least they would eat an organic hamburger without the bun), not to mention the burgeoning foodie-ism, my proposed menu would have been unthinkable, even if I could have persuaded Eric to go along with it – which would have been impossible. Even those who might have really wanted to eat the juicy burgers would never have allowed their friends to see them imbibing. As for beer, well Yuppies just don't do beer – at least they didn't until beer tasting parties recently started to move up the coolness scale, but that's another story for another day.

You might well ask how I knew that this was in fact an invitation for a barbeque. Well, on the folded part of the invitation card facing the engraved type there was a cartoon picture of a smiling chef wearing a silly apron as he leaned over a smoking grill. So I had my answer to the first puzzle of just what she meant by alfresco dining 'experience.' The next puzzle that had to be solved was precisely what Renée would mean by the term 'casual.' Was she trying to trick us? Trip us up? Casual had to mean something that I must have been overlooking because Eric told me that I'd probably need a new outfit. In general terms, I wasn't opposed on principle to shopping for a new outfit, but I was fairly certain that I had scads of 'casual' clothes therefore wouldn't have a clue where to look for something that would meet Renée's criteria for 'casual.'

Would I go to a sports store? Perhaps Banana Republic? The Gap? Help me out here, I had to say to Eric. Could I just troll the mall to find a new sweater? At that last suggestion he was aghast. Not the mall! So it was off to boutique land I went.

With Eric's expert assistance, I was able to find what he called "just the right sort of outfit for effect." What effect? I did ask him that very question in the store, but I never did get an answer. Perhaps he thought it was a rhetorical question. That seemed to happen a lot in our interactions in those days.

My estimate of the effect he was looking for would probably have been "this is expensive." To that end, I appeared at the barbeque in the most expensive 'casual' outfit that I had ever or have since owned. However, I was certainly not alone. Several of the women came wearing designer swimsuits with matching cover-ups that looked like filmy, colorful cocktail dresses. The effect was like being inside a butterfly exhibition.

Renée had not been wrong in calling this an 'experience.' Predictably, the menu did not consist of any of the usual, familiar BBQ foods that were so much a part of my childhood. Rather the gargantuan, stainless-steel BBQ itself spent the entire party huddled under its black vinyl cover. The caterers brought a wide assortment of gastronomic delights that the servers kept telling people were prepared on a real barbeque back at their kitchen downtown.

We began with hot hors d'oeuvres. The first trays to come out were laden with mushrooms stuffed with pancetta and goat cheese that I had begun to chew before the waiter informed us of their contents. Then there were goat cheese tarts – goat cheese was very on-trend that season, but I had, unfortunately, never been able to develop a taste for it. In fact, the smell often made me feel queasy.

As Eric took a tart off the tray and began to nibble, I whispered, "You don't really like that, do you?" This was one food that we agreed on.

"For god's sake, Alex, it's polite to try."

"Even if they make me gag?"

"Well, everyone else seems to like them," he said looking around the yard as if other people liking them made a difference to my gag reflex – or his.

He was right. Everyone else seemed to be 'oohing' and 'ahhing' over the food which didn't seem substantial enough for my expectations for a barbeque.

After those memorable starters, we were treated to the salad course. Renee had set up a half a dozen tables festooned with white table cloths and fresh flowers. On the buffet table set up on the patio was radicchio salad – another food that made me gag. I had no doubt that the dressing was made from tofu or some other such tasteless substance. I took a small bit and moved it around on my plate for a while until the waiters brought in the main course.

It was beet linguini covered with some kind of bright green sauce which immediately put me in the Christmas spirit – all that red and green floating around on the plates. The only reason I was able to identify the sources of the red color in the pasta was that I had heard Renée discussing interminably at several cocktail parties her personal search for precisely the right ingredients for home-made pasta and its variations. This made me wonder if she had actually made the pasta herself. She had opined that beet pasta was her all-time favorite, but when I tasted it, I thought it tasted like boxed spaghetti that had been buried in the ground for an entire winter, dug up in the spring and served without even the courtesy of a thorough washing. I guess I was a Neanderthal when it came to food because right about then I was longing for a steak on the BBQ.

I really don't remember much else about the party – I guess it was supposed to be all about the food anyway. I do remember suffering from indigestion for the following two days, and so did Eric, although he wouldn't admit it. I saw the antacid wrappers in the waste basket in the bathroom, though.

~

All of these memories of parties past, and Renée's involvement, made me wonder what was going on in her life now. Although I had realized ever since that ski date with her husband that things were not as rosy as she suggested, I had never really given much thought to the extent of their problems. I wondered if they were at all related to Renée's recent return to the world of the working woman – or perhaps Robert had been straying just a fraction too far.

Anyway I didn't really have time to spend considering other people's problems: I had enough of my own. Juggling a briefcase, dry cleaning and liquor bottles, I struggled to open the front door when I finally pulled into the driveway without incident. I tried to wave at my neighbors Patty, a newbie lawyer and her husband Andy, an accountant as they ran by waving. Typical of newbie Yuppies, they had told us that they planned to have two children when they could find "an appropriate window" in Patty's career ladder. Good luck with that, I had thought at the time. I supposed it would happen when she got tired of being a junior associate at her current law firm and couldn't see a promotion to partner anywhere on the horizon. They went running at precisely 5:30 pm four afternoons a week. Today they were wearing what appeared to be new lululemon outfits: his was black shorts with a sky blue singlet; hers was black shorts with a fuchsia yoga tank. They were so cute.

I tried to wave back by putting the liquor store bag under my arm, but immediately stopped myself when it appeared as if the bottles might crash onto the concrete step at any moment. I wished that I had their motivation. It was all I could do to drag myself to the gym for an aerobics class three times a week. I had managed to deflect any and all attempts by my friends to get me to join them in hot yoga classes. I shook my head wondering when that particular fad would come to an end. Right now in the heat, all I could think about was getting inside and running a cool bath. Isobel had called me on the way home to suggest we have a pre-party drink downtown before the party. I had agreed to meet her.

As I walked into the kitchen and put the bags of wine on the counter I noticed two of Eric's jackets that he'd asked me to take to the cleaners were still neatly folded on the back of a bar stool. Rats! (I actually thought, shit, but that's not so nice.) He would be livid – in that sort of controlled way that he had. It occurred to me that I'd take them with me when I went downtown to meet Isobel, so scooped them up so that the evidence of my negligence wouldn't be in Eric's face when he arrived home. I didn't want to start off our anniversary celebrations on such a sour note.

Before I stuffed them into an empty grocery bag, I automatically put my hand in the pockets to check for forgotten items as I always did before taking anything to the drycleaner. Not expecting to find anything, I was surprised when my fingers touched something in the left inside breast pocket of his gray Burberry blazer. To my utter astonishment, I pulled out two ticket stubs – to a night club to which Eric had never gone in his life. At least as far as I knew he had never set foot in the place.

I sat down on the bar stool and put them on the counter. The black ticket stubs stood out against the white granite of the counter top. Did Eric have secrets, too? The very idea was delicious to me. I suppose I should have been shocked as the oblivious wife, but my reaction was quite the contrary. This could be the most interesting thing I'd learned about my husband for many years. But I supposed that he probably had a logical explanation for their presence in his pocket. I would never have suspected such a thing of Eric, and I would have especially never have dreamed that he'd appear at such a place. As far as I knew, the patrons were considerably younger than Eric. I really only knew about it from a brief conversation I'd had with Pam in the coffee room at work one day several months earlier. As shy as she seemed to be, she had gone there unwillingly, at least according to her, one

Saturday night to a stagette. I remembered her saying that it was quite an expensive place.

I contemplated the date on the stubs. June 8. Puzzling over this for a moment, I looked at the calendar hanging inside a kitchen cupboard door. Eric was always meticulous about noting where he'd be on this, our co-operative calendar, so that I wouldn't double-book him in an evening. He had a horror of double-booking.

According to our calendar, he had noted a regional dental association meeting that evening. I remembered that he'd been out that evening because it had afforded me the opportunity to finish a manuscript that my editor was waiting for. I usually had to do that work in the office, but that evening I remembered pouring myself a glass of Malbec and happily writing my way into my imagination. I remembered, because I had emailed it to my editor the next day and was expecting it to bounce back any day for revisions. I made a mental note to check my email before I got into the bath.

I had never been in the habit of checking up on Eric's whereabouts in the past: he had always been precisely where he said he'd be. At least I thought he had. There had never seemed to be even the slightest need to doubt him. Should I have been more astute? I was baffled. It would have been so out of character for Eric to do something like this – and neglect to mention it to me. If he were trying to

84

hide something from me he would have remembered to remove the ticket stubs from his pocket – he was that sort of person who never missed a detail. Did he want me to find them? I was beginning to feel like a character on an afternoon soap. Did he? Would he? Should I? Shouldn't I? The whole thing gave me a headache so I headed off to my bath, checking my email on the way – and there it was, winking at me from my laptop on top of my dresser. My latest manuscript with my editor's first-pass edits. As always, the thought made me tingle, but I didn't have time to get to it before the evening festivities. It would have to wait.

SIX

A warm bath with lots of bubbles – that was just what I needed. This was my thought as I slid down into the enveloping warmth. Then I reached for my phone which was never far from my hand and started to dictate...

Olivia slid down into the pink bubbles of the enormous jetted tub in the hotel's penthouse suite. Her mind wandered to the hour just spent in the adjoining bedroom. Yes, she thought, he was just as chiseled here as he seemed to be on the court earlier today. I knew I had to have him, she thought, and I was right. As she sank beneath the bubbles, she heard him call her name. He was waiting for her to return to his arms. But she wanted to spend just a moment longer remembering the nuances of his touch so different from that of his opponent. What (or who) is next, she thought as she slid slowly above the bubbles. She lifted her well-toned leg and began to drip sudsy water that dripped languidly down toward her center just as he appeared, fully naked, in the door. She could see that he was ready...

The damn doorbell started to ring just as I was getting to what I considered to be the heart of my stories. I hated to be interrupted mid-thought. Interruption or not, god herself could not have gotten me out of the bathtub at that moment. I placed the phone back on the side of the tub and spent a few more moments hoping that the insistent bell-ringer would go away. Eventually it stopped and several moments later I heard Eric's voice.

I was somewhat pleased with myself for having come to a decision about the ticket stubs, because I had. I supposed that knowing Eric as I had for the past decade plus, it was unlikely that there was anything at all sinister about their presence. They probably weren't even his. Thus I had decided to be the bigger person and simply ask him about them directly rather than sneaking around checking up on him. I would do it subtly, though.

Eric was calling my name from below as usual. Eventually he made it upstairs and rapped on the door just as I noticed that my fingers were beginning to resemble prunes – or Eric's mother's face.

"Alex, did you manage to finish all the errands on the list?"

Not even a hello. This was my cue to pretend that I was either washing my hair or cleaning the bath tub. I noisily turned on the faucet and pretended that I couldn't hear him.

He knocked harder. "Alex!" Louder this time.

I was now out of the tub wrapped in a large fluffy white towel. I turned on my hairdryer. He banged on the door again. I waited an appropriate length of time – or so I thought – and emerged from the bathroom.

"Oh, Eric," I said, "I didn't hear you come in. You're early. How was your day? Mrs. Goldfarb's teeth give you any trouble?"

"My day was fine, and it's no wonder you can't hear anything with all that racket you're making in there." He started rummaging in his closet. "And why are *you* getting ready so early? You never like to sit around all done up as you say. We don't have to be at the party for hours."

"I'm meeting Isobel downtown for a drink in about a half hour. We haven't had a chance to chat for ages. I watched as Eric painstakingly examined very piece of clothing in the dry cleaning. "Do you recognize that blue sweater on the hanger next to the canvas pants? It looks familiar to me, but I don't remember ever seeing you in it. Is it yours?"

"It is a woman's sweater," he continued without waiting for me to answer. "It certainly isn't my sweater. Well, you better stop at the drycleaner on your way to see Isobel and take it back. Someone is probably missing it."

He unloaded the pockets of his clinic jacket which he was still wearing. He placed their contents on his dresser beside the ticket stubs that I

88

had placed there with the objective of starting a conversation. If he noticed them (which he could not have missed) he decided to ignore them.

"Eric, do you really want to go to this party tonight? It's going to be a rerun of every single party we've been to over the last ten years. It's our anniversary. Couldn't we just spend it here? Talking?"

"Talking? About what? We can't stay here. We're the guests of honor."

"But these parties are so boring. No one knows how to just have a good time anymore. Everyone's so concerned that they're doing all the right things. Whatever those are." My voice trailed off.

"I think you're paying far too much attention to things that Isobel is talking about. Maybe you should cancel your drink date with her this evening."

"Eric, I really want to see Isobel. No matter what you might think of her, she's been a great friend to me over the years."

He sighed. "Whatever. How long is it going to take you to get made up?"

"About twenty minutes. I have to wrestle my hair into some kind of submission and do my make-up."

"I'm going to change and have a glass of something myself," he said undoing his belt. "I don't suppose there's anything to eat?"

Ducking back into the bathroom, I pretended not to hear him. Good lord, he could open a cupboard himself, couldn't he?

The sound of the hairdryer drowned out everything for about ten minutes. When I turned it off, I heard Eric's steps going down the stairs. I moved on to makeup and emerged from the bathroom fifteen minutes later looking at least presentable. I must have been too focused on my ablutions to hear Eric come back upstairs, because when I noticed him, he was sitting in the wing chair by the window holding a glass of what looked like scotch. I drew this conclusion from the fact that the bottle was on the floor next to him. This was odd behavior since Eric wasn't really that much of a drinker, especially not of hard liquor. Wine was usually his drug of choice.

We exchanged a few inanities about the hot weather as I got dressed, but I couldn't help noticing that Eric was acting somewhat odd, even for him. What in the world was he up to, I wondered?

He downed the first glass and poured himself another – it was going to be a very long evening, I thought. Just then, he burped. Loudly. It was not one of his usual polite gee-I'm-really-sorry-excuse-me kind of burp. No, it was an earth-quake-causing belch that I'd heard only once before on some kind of reality show where the men all wear do-rags and spend their days in swamps or mud-pits or some such thing. After more than ten years of intimate contact with this man sitting before me, I had never yet heard such a sound emanate from his lips. I decided to ignore it. Besides, how do you really respond to something like that? And something so out of character?

He looked at his watch. "You better hurry if you don't want to be late."

Clearly, but for no apparent reason, he had changed his mind about the prudence of my drink-date with Isobel. I must have given him an odd look, because never in his life had he been concerned that I hurry anywhere to meet Isobel. In fact, he usually continued to try to talk me out of it even as I walked out the door brandishing car keys. I was beginning to wonder what was going on. It couldn't be...no, it couldn't be that he had an anniversary surprise for me, did he?

"Are you feeling all right?" I said.

"Of course, darling. I'm feeling wonderful. Never better." He drained the second glass. "Really, it is awfully hot today, isn't it?"

Enough about the weather, I thought.

I finished dressing and headed downstairs with him following along behind me. He poured another glass of scotch – his third by my count. "You might want to take it easy on the booze so early in the evening," I said. "Did something happen today? Should we talk about it?"

In spite of the fact that I really didn't want to talk to him right that moment, it occurred to me that there could be something really important to have this kind of effect on him. Or maybe he was just hot.

"Whatever gave you that idea, my darling?"

Two 'my darlings' in one evening? Now I was really beginning to get suspicious.

"I just have a few things to do before the party," he was saying as he retrieved a glass of fresh ice from the dispenser on the refrigerator door. "You go ahead and enjoy your little girl-talk rendezvous. It'll give me a chance to get those few things done. Nothing for you to be concerned about. Go on, you don't want to be late."

I didn't have time to continue discussing the matter with him, as peculiar as it was to hear him encouraging me to see Isobel. I just hoped that he'd be somewhat lucid when I got home. Judging from the volume of scotch he had downed, coupled with his low capacity for alcohol, lucidity was not a certainty. So, I left him in the company of a glass of water with a scotch chaser and headed downtown to meet Isobel.

It was our plan to meet at the *Santa Lucia Bar & Bistro*. For years it had been our favorite meeting place primarily because we were unlikely to see any of Eric's friends or acquaintances there. It was what Eric would have called a 'dive', but they made wonderful cappuccino and champagne cocktails. Who could argue with that? Whenever either of us was feeling a bit down over the years, we'd meet for a gab and a flute of champagne over a cognac-drenched sugar cube. Wonderful!

The main problem with the bistro though, was that there was a distinct lack of parking resulting in the requirement to walk about four blocks unless you were extremely lucky. In any case, I reached the *Santa Lucia* before Isobel and found a seat near a window where there was a slight breeze. All of the outside tables were jammed with people sipping various beers and fanning themselves with menus.

The waitress approached looking as hot as I felt. "A beer perhaps?" she said.

"That would be wonderful," I said.

I was thinking about beer as I scanned the menu. As I mentioned, no one in our circle of friends actually drank beer – at least not until recently. It was considered too déclassé for most of them until it started to develop its own kind of pretentious caché. After several of Eric's nearest and dearest read an article about 'cicerones', beer took on a whole new status. You might well ask: what in the world is a cicerone? And that would be a very good question.

It seems that a cicerone is to beer what a sommelier is to wine. And group beer-tasting parties have even started to enter into the line-up of entertainment for Yuppies. Of course, anyone who loves a beer at a hockey game or with a burger on the deck on a summer evening doesn't really need anyone to tell him which beers have what kind of subtle flavors. He chooses what he likes from the beer store. But Eric's friends seem to want a more nuanced approach. Thankfully, the *Santa Lucia Café and Bar* did not employ the services of a cicerone; rather they had two types of beer on tap and three or four in bottles. That's all anyone who came in ever needed.

As I sipped my beer, enjoying its icy coldness as it slid down my throat, I gazed around at the happy crowd here. It wasn't the sort of place any of our so-called friends would spend any time. With its slightly fading and peeling wallpaper and its white wrought-iron tables and chairs, it was a kind of down-market establishment that had yet to be touched by the hand of the gentrification squad like so much of the older parts of the city had. It was a place that many local artists and actors came to sit for long periods of time and contemplate whatever artists contemplated. And there was always a group of university students to generate some rowdiness in the evenings. I sighed that kind of depressed sigh that occasionally signals my contemplation of my lost artist. I found myself more and more frequently longing for a simpler life where I could dress as I liked and spend my life pursuing only my creative side. But I also knew that the life of the starving artist wasn't as glamorous as it looked from the outside. I knew that many of them struggled day to day. That realization always made me feel a tad better about my Yuppie choices – as bad as I was at them.

While I waited for Isobel, I started to tap out a few passages on my tablet.

Olivia was tired of tennis players, and hockey players, and football players. They had been the first phase of her exploration. Now, it was time for artists. And today was her first day. Never before had this life drawing class had such a sensuous life model, she thought. The school – all boys – had liked her résumé, and Olivia had liked the idea of ten young men spending two hours admiring the form and function of her body that she had so lovingly created over the years. Reclined as she was on the ruby red of the velvet cushions scattered

95

on the floor of the light-filled studio, she could feel their reverence. Their gazes were like cool breezes caressing her bare limbs. Desire filled the room like a palpable presence. All ten were flushed with yearning, and she could see from the corner of her eye that the teacher was not immune either. He stood slightly to the side watching not his charges; rather his gaze was fixed on Olivia. And so they sketched while the breeze caressing her limbs began to warm until it was too hot to handle. The bell rang and they filed out, eyes longingly fixed on her as she slid into the silk gown. Only one remained. Their artist-teacher was there to offer his hand. As the door closed, the robe began to slip...

I stopped typing and slid the tablet into my over-sized and altogether too heavy tote bag under the table. I was still deep in thought about Olivia and what (or more to the point who) she would do next. I was still contemplating this delicious idea when Isobel bounced into the seat across from me flinging her bulging briefcase under her chair.

"Jeezus, Alex, daydreaming again? If Eric catches you, he'll have you committed!" She said, laughing.

She had seen me in deep contemplation before – never knowing what I was thinking about, I might add – and she had also seen Eric's response to me. Not pretty.

Anyway, Isobel brought me quickly back to my other reality. I smiled at this thought, as well as the usual incongruity between the prim, professional brown leather of her briefcase and her completely non-lawyerly attire. Not a fan of the dignified, conventional sartorial choices of her colleagues in the legal profession, Isobel was a bit of a rebel. Early on in her career she had made a conscious decision that she would not be a clone of every other female lawyer on Bay Street, most of whom busied themselves trying to be a clone of the pin-striped men. She was horrified when Brooks Brothers opened a store in the city. I know this because she had moaned to me about it on more than one occasion.

Isobel was an individualist in her dress as much as she was in her selection of men she dated. I wondered who she was bringing to the party tonight, but decided that if she didn't offer a description I would rather be surprised. If past occasions were any clue, it just might be the highlight of the evening.

"Are you and Eric ready for another wild evening at the Rubenstein mansion?" Isobel could not talk about her cousin Rebecca without dripping sarcasm. Oh, I didn't tell you that they were cousins, did I?

"I could seriously live without it, but Eric as usual insists that it's important."

"Well, you are the guests of honor tonight." She beckoned toward the waiter. "Eric does seem to always want to go to these parties, but if you ask me, when he gets there he always looks as though he'd rather be anywhere else. He's never been a real party animal, you know, Alex."

I snorted. "Party animal? Certainly not! Well, maybe tonight will be a first," I muttered, cooling my hands on the beer glass.

"Something amiss in the little love nest you call home?"

"Not sure. Eric was drunk when I left the house to meet you."

Isobel's eyes began to pop, and then she laughed out loud. "Good for him! Maybe he's learning to let his hair down." The waiter set a beer glass in front of her. She raised it as if in a toast. "Here's to a new and potentially improved Dr. Eric Harvey!"

We clunked glasses and sipped while mopping sweat off our brows.

"Why today, though, Alex? Did he have some kind of an epiphany?"

"That's what I'd like to know," I said. I decided to run my theory by Isobel. "I think he may be having an affair."

98

"You can't be serious? Boring old Eric? It would be the most interesting thing he's done in ten years."

I probably wouldn't have taken that response from anyone but Isobel to whom I felt no obligation to defend my husband. She knew him almost as well as I did. She understood our relationship – or at least she used to.

"Ouch," I said. "I know it sounds too weird to be true, but there is some evidence." I told her about the ticket stubs."

"Purely circumstantial," the lawyer was saying. "Innocent until proven guilty. Besides, I usually hear that kind of gossip and there hasn't been a word."

Isobel was right – she did hear gossip. For all her complaints about the Yuppie world I lived in and that she tried to avoid, she was totally plugged into what was going on. She might have worked in a legal aid office without the fancy trimmings, but several of her colleagues were Yuppies-who-protest-too-much –about-not-being-Yuppies. And they knew what was going on in my particular circle of Yuppies.

"Just imagine," she continued, "stuffy old Dr. Harvey having a torrid love affair with some young tart. I suppose he does it at the office in his dental chair. Maybe they use the electronic maneuvers to best advantage!"

By the time Isobel finished her parody of the dental chair love affair, we both had tears of laughter streaming down our faces and other patrons were beginning to look at us disapprovingly.

"You know, Alex," Isobel said when she finally had control again, "you should write to J.L. Kidston. She could probably use some of this stuff for a book about the promiscuous dentist."

I didn't even blanche at her words. It wouldn't be the first time that old J.L. had gotten a story idea from Isobel. I only hoped that she had never noticed.

"What makes you think J.L. Kidston is a woman?" I asked nonchalantly.

"Elementary, my dear Alex. All of her main protagonists are women. No man could write about the female orgasm that accurately! Anyway, her heroines really capture the physical and emotional sensations of a woman involved in a relationship."

I was feeling flattered and trying hard not to show it. Isobel had no idea.

"You see," she continued, "I believe that J.L. is writing mainly autobiographical books."

"May I remind you that even '50 Shades of Grey' wasn't written as autobiography."

"True. But that's where J.L. and E.L. differ. J.L. is so much more authentic. At least that's the way I see it."

I knew that someday I was going to have to come clean with Isobel, and I sometimes wondered why I hadn't done it yet. She could keep a secret, and she would be very upset to know that I'd kept this secret from her for so long. It would be nice to be able to discuss my writing with someone other than my agent and my editor, both of whom had too much vested interest in what I wrote. I often thought that the bottom line clouded their judgment. Maybe I should self-publish – but that was something to think about at another time.

"You know that book J.L. wrote about the goings on behind the scenes in a PR firm? I really thought you should have written it. From what you've told me, with your background and me putting in the sex scenes, I'll bet we could give J.L. a run for her money. I'll bet we could steal half her readership!"

Interesting idea. But J. L. really didn't need a writing partner. Not yet, anyway.

SEVEN

Isobel was still waxing on about writing ideas for her (and presumably my) erotic novel when I spotted two men sitting at the next table. The reason they stood out was that they were wearing name tags. You know the kind – those large, plasticised ones proclaiming one's name and affiliation worn around the neck on a lanyard adorned with some company or other's logo. They were clearly attending a convention and couldn't have seen fit to take off the name tags before escaping. I cringed slightly. There were few things about conventions I liked less than the name tags, unless it was wearing name tags while not actually attending a convention-related event.

In the early years of our marriage, Eric hadn't been much of what you'd call a 'joiner.' But something happened right around our first anniversary. I don't know what came over him, but he became a card-carrying member of more than one dental association (who knew that there were so many special-interest dental topics around which dentists clustered?) and found it necessary to actively support several. This support inevitably resulted in the need to attend at least one tax-deductible convention each year and presto! A vacation for Alex. Not so much.

Eric had often also opined that it might be a terrific idea to get himself appointed as national representative to one or more international dental associations (international teeth, anyone?) so that he could travel free of charge outside the country at least twice a year. Of course, I was more than welcome to come along, then there would be no need to budget for other vacations, and he'd have an endless supply of travel anecdotes, a necessity for his Yuppie reputation.

The first time Eric began regular attendance at out-of-town conventions I stayed home. Not that I wanted to go anyway – I had never really been that keen on social situations populated by dentists – but I did have a client pitch that we'd been working on for some months. The timing was just off. However, when he returned, his ravings made me realize that it wouldn't be so easy to get out of it the next year like all the other dutiful dental spouses. I would be attending at his side. The fact that I might have other commitments just didn't wash. So, I obediently put aside my own work the next year and that first convention was an experience that will be forever seared on my brain.

~

There is no experience, I believe, that compares with spending four nights and four days with 150 dentists and their spouses. Excuse me; I should

103

have said spouse/guests since that's what the nametags said. Back in the "olden days" when most dentists were men (that is decidedly not the case any longer), wives were expected to attend these things and did so without question. Eric was a bit of an anachronism in that respect. Yes, we had to wear name tags. I am most definitely not a name tag kind of girl, but wear one I did.

When we arrived at the hotel in downtown Montreal – two hours behind schedule since there had been snow (when in the winter does it not snow in Montreal?) – we were greeted by a lobby full of what were clearly dentists and their spouse/partner/guests. There was much furtive glancing around – I'm not sure why, since the days of comparing Rolex watches were over, or so I thought. But at that point one couldn't really tell who was a conventioneer or not – the inescapable name tags had not yet appeared. They would come later at the welcome reception.

Name tag or no name tag, Eric began scouting around.

"Who are you looking for?" I asked, shifting my tote bag from one shoulder to another.

"Just looking for a couple of my classmates who come to these things every year; and there were a few people I met last year I thought you should meet."

I could not even imagine who I "should" meet, not to mention anyone I'd really like to meet. Oh well, I thought, I'm being really bitchy and these just might be the nicest people ever. Why was I so prejudiced? Why did I have such negative preconceptions? Oh yes, I remembered. It was based on several dismal dinners I'd had with Eric's dentist friends at home. These events had been emblazoned in my mind as musts-to-avoid at all costs. And here I was, about to embark on dentist immersion super-sized. In for a penny…

Just as we were about to reach the front of the hotel check-in line, Eric caught sight of a familiar face. Grabbing my arm, he jerked me out of the line toward a couple who were wrestling their bags off the bellman's cart.

"Chuck!" he began as he slapped a short, porky-looking man on the back. "Good to see you again. You're looking well."

I didn't think Chuck looked especially well. In fact, the way he way huffing and puffing over those two suitcases I thought he might have a cardiac event at any moment.

"Chuck, I'd like you to meet my wife, Alexis."

Oh, so we were being formal this weekend, were we? Eric never called me Alexis except in two sets of circumstances. One was when he was trying to put on airs with people; the other was when he was annoyed at me. Exceedingly. It was very likely the former in this instance.

"Alexis," he said reaching out to shake my hand. At least I thought he was going to shake my hand until the moment when I found myself cheek to sweaty cheek while he planted a large kiss on my neck. He smelled slightly of some musky aftershave mingled with a soupçon of tobacco, finished off with a lingering dash of B.O. I held my breath until he released me.

"Chuck," I said when I was finally able to take a fresh breath again, "delighted." I turned to the woman next to him. "And you must be Chuck's wife."

"Well, I do prefer to be identified independently, but yes. I'm Sheridan. Dr. Sheridan Walters. I'm a gynecologist. I specialize in fertility treatment. Perhaps you've seen me on television?"

I hadn't. Okay, I thought. Just a bit too much information for a first acquaintance. Was I supposed to be impressed? Simply put her in a pigeon hole? Conclude that she made lots of money? I only thought of the latter because I had already had plenty of experience with Eric's friends who did provide this kind of information so that others could be impressed and consider the financial success that must accompany such credentials. I wasn't very good at feigning being impressed. I just smiled and told her that I was Alex and that I was pleased to meet her. My smile was beginning to feel forced.

"I'm surprised that you've been able to take the time off from your medical practice to take in this convention," I heard myself saying.

Eric frowned slightly. Perhaps he thought I was being sarcastic. I wasn't. I was truly surprised.

"I always come," Sheridan said. "Chuck and I do everything together...except work!"

I looked at Chuck who was now wiping sweat off his brow with what appeared to be a cloth handkerchief and stuffing it back in his breast pocket. Then I looked at Sheridan who did, in fact look like she just stepped off a television shoot. She was impeccable in what appeared to be an actual Chanel suit that fit her as if it had been made-to-measure – which it probably was. Her nude-colored pumps had a three-inch heels and a slight platform – and that distinctive red sole was clearly visible. She carried a large, black quilted Chanel tote bag. Oh, and did I mention that she was at least two inches taller than Chuck? Well, who was I to judge. The eye of the beholder, and all. But I did wonder how such an impeccably groomed woman could be happy with someone who smelled like Chuck did close up. Perhaps those were the pheromones to which she was attracted.

Eric and I finally did get registered and had found our way up on the elevator without too much interference by other convention-goers. Once we had unpacked we got ourselves registered for the convention, taking our tote bags full of swag provided by a plethora of dental companies along with us to dinner where we plotted out the next few days.

Eric really didn't care if I attended any of the spouse/guest activities or not. I was free to go shopping on my own, to chill out at the spa or tour a museum or two. He had only one major stipulation – that I attend all of the group social functions with him. I agreed.

The highlight of the weekend was the dinner held at the Versailles Ballroom at Le Windsor. Lined with Corinthian columns, the massive space was filled with snowy-white-tablecloth-topped tables that were set with twinkling crystal and china. As I looked around and upward, I was rewarded by the sight of a magnificent gilded ceiling. At that moment, I was happy that I had decided to pull out all the stops this evening and wear my most formal Yuppie-approved cocktail dress.

As the evening progressed, I was even more impressed that the venue had been able to pull off a wonderful meal for the 300 people assembled and expecting rubber chicken. Instead of the usual conference fare, and keeping with the decidedly French theme (And why not? We were, after all, in Montreal!), we were treated to a choice of *canard à l'orange* (duck), *escalopes de veau à la crème* (veal cutlets with mushrooms and cream), or *poulet au porto* (chicken steeped in port). It was as if the chef were channeling Julia Child! I was in heaven as I savoured the first bites of my *poulet* accompanied by *champignons à la grecque* (face it – I'd eat mushrooms even if they weren't à la grecque!).

And so the dinner was progressing magnificently when the usual conversation – that I'd hoped Eric might skip this time – started up in earnest.

"What kind of car you driving these days, Eric?" Ron began.

Ron was sitting across the table from me beside his mousy wife whose name I can't now remember – all I do remember was that she talked of nothing else but her children's private school. I winced slightly knowing that Eric would now be off and running – or driving.

"Oh, I picked up a new Beemer recently. You?"

Picked up?? Eric had spent the better part of a year pouring over glossy brochures of every high-end car manufactured outside North America. He then set up a schedule and methodically test-drove

109

each one over a period of three months keeping meticulous notes on his phone, notes he reviewed over and over with me although it never occurred to him that I might not care what kind of car he bought. I didn't. Then, as you would if you were picking out a house, he selected a short list and went back for a second look – and drive. I could not understand why it was so hard to pick out a car. You set your budget, decided what kind of options you can't live without and just pick one. At least that had always been my point of view.

"I finally broke down and bought myself that Porsche I've been salivating over since dental school. Not very practical, I know, but Cheryl has the station wagon – a Volvo."

That was her name! Cheryl was beaming from one bejewelled ear to another as her beloved Ron, whom I did remember was a classmate of Eric's, raved on about his sports car. Mid-life crisis anyone? A bit early in my view, though.

RON: (to Eric) How's your practice going these days? (Translation: How much money are you making?)

ERIC: (to Ron) Couldn't be better! (Translation: I'm raking in the money.)

RON: (to Eric) Sounds great. I had to take an extra vacation last year just to get a break from the patients. And to keep the income tax down! *laughs* (Translation: I'm making more money than you are…and I can afford the real toys like the Porsche).

My jaw started to clench. These kinds of conversations followed me around wherever I was it seemed these days. Who cares how your income stacks up against that of your colleagues, friends, neighbors, enemies? Just as they all finished discussing their latest toys, and just as the conversation was beginning to turn to vacation destinations, Cheryl's head popped back up from under the table where she had evidently been searching the contents of her evening bag. She didn't keep us in suspense for a moment longer.

"Anyone have any dental floss?"

Before you could say "Emily Post" four packages had materialized on the table top and were offered to her to rescue her from what must have been enormous discomfort to have even mentioned dental floss at a formal dinner. But I wasn't surprised.

I thought (hoped) that she would select one and excuse herself from the table to floss in private. Unfortunately, that was more than could be expected from a dental wife, and I knew it from bitter experience. She picked up a package of spearmint-flavored floss, thanked the giver, tore off a piece and proceeded to floss the offending tooth. I closed my eyes for a split second, and in that brief interval, another of the dentists at the table had reached across and picked up another of the packages.

Tearing off a long piece for himself, he said, "Don't mind if I do," then uttered a mild expletive or two about the "damned chicken."

I excused myself and fled to the ladies' room before I upchucked over the lot of them. This was an affectation of the dental community that I had never been able to understand among people with otherwise acceptable table manners.

~

"Alex? Earth to Alex!" Isobel was waving her hand in front of my face, bringing me abruptly back from my mental walk down memory lane.

"Hmm?" I shook myself back to reality.

"Alex, do you see those two men over there wearing name tags?"

I looked in the direction that she was trying not to gesture. She seemed to be pointing my attention to the two men whose presence had induced my reverie in the first place.

"They would make a fascinating pair of characters for a novel don't you think?"

I was beginning to wonder if Isobel was baiting me – perhaps she knew more about my secret life than I thought. Since I wasn't yet ready to spill about it to anyone, I was going to have to be more careful.

112

"Well," I said considering my thoughts, "all they really did for me was to remind me of all those boring dental conventions I've suffered through for the past ten years. By the way," I said neatly changing the subject, "who are you bringing to the party tonight? I can stand the suspense no longer!" I had changed my mind about not asking her the question.

"Actually, I'm bringing a new man."

No surprise there. "Anyone I know?"

"Not likely. In fact, I doubt if anyone will know him, which means that I'll have to entertain him the whole evening. Not really a bad situation, though. He's very cute.'

"Are you going to tell me about him or do I have to guess?"

She stuck out her tongue at me like we used to do when we were kids together. "I met him on a flight back from New York a couple of months ago. He's an editor for a New York publisher that has offices here."

I snorted a bit of beer up into my nose then had to try desperately to be nonchalant about this revelation.

"Here," she said handing me a napkin. "Anyway, he's a bit older than I am – quite a bit actually, but that's what makes him so fascinating. You know, come to think of it, he looks a bit like

Paul Newman in his earlier days." She looked at me. "Don't give me that face."

I'm not exactly sure what kind of face she was seeing, but I sincerely hoped that it wasn't the face I was feeling as our conversation inched ever closer to my secret territory. Surely it couldn't be anyone in my own publishing sphere despite the fact that I had thought that very thing about my own editor whose name actually happened to be Paul. "So, what's his name?"

"You won't know it. He's not famous. After all, editors are the unsung heroes of the publishing business, you know. Where would writers be without editors?"

A lot richer, I was thinking. "Perhaps editors would be a bit less unsung if anyone actually gave out their names," I ventured.

"His name is Paul Cameron and he actually edits erotic novels. I think that's why I've been so focused on them lately." Isobel looked very pleased with herself as if somehow editing those novels translated into behaviour in other spheres of his life. I, on the other hand, thought I might actually choke.

The air in the room seemed to be sucked out as if by some alien source; I was certain that I was seeing stars. "Does he ever talk about his authors?" I said when I finally found my voice.

"Not really. Although I do know that his company publishes J.L. Kidston's books. When he told me that I thought I was dreaming. He started up the conversation when he noticed I was reading one in actual book format. I guess she sells a lot of electronic books these days. I had dinner with him while he was here, and when he told me that he'd be back this week, I asked him if he'd like to come to the party. I was kind of surprised when he said yes. I think he'll add a bit of class to Rebecca's little shindig tonight!"

I hoped that the faintness I was feeling wasn't apparent to Isobel, but she did seem to be somewhat smitten and a bit in her own world. I had no idea that Paul was in town, and I wondered what he was doing in Toronto. He worked mainly in New York, and in fact in all the years he'd been editing my books, we had conducted our face-to-face meetings in New York. Feeling a bit territorial, I was experiencing what seemed to be jealousy that Isobel was spending more time with my own editor than I was. Maybe he had brought my updated contract for the next book. This couldn't be it, though, since my identity had been religiously guarded under the terms of my contract, and we usually conducted all of our business electronically. Paul and I had maintained a very close and productive working relationship through the years, and now I would be faced with hoping that nothing this evening would give away our relationship. Would I be able to pretend that I was meeting him for the first time? Would he?

"He sounds nice, Isobel. Do you think the relationship is going anywhere? I mean, it's tough to have a long-distance love affair."

"He's in town to see a piece of lakefront property. I think he may be planning to make a move up here to take over the Canadian branch of the publishing house. Isn't that exciting? Then it wouldn't be long-distance, would it?" She took a sip of her beer. "But seriously, I'm not sure he's my type. He's very nice and very handsome, but he's a bit too corporate for me. He's not really enough of a free spirit, but I'll reserve judgment until I get to know him a bit better. It should be fun to see him with all those Yuppie friends of yours tonight!"

Funny thing, I'd often had lustful thoughts about Paul myself. What I was feeling was an odd mixture of abject terror and, oddly, protectiveness. On more than one occasion I had fantasized about the two of us together – even before his recent divorce. (I wondered if he had told Isobel about that little part of his background.)

Isobel checked her watch.

"Yikes," she said, "I have to go if I'm going to be ready when Paul comes to pick me up. He's never been to my condo so I'll have to tidy up a bit." She stood up, hoisting her large tote over her

116

shoulder then leaned to give me a hug. "Happy anniversary, kid! See you later!"

With that she was gone. I decided to stay just a bit longer and have a glass of iced tea before I made my way home to a drunken husband. Dear god, I thought, what would tonight bring?

After Isobel left, I sat for a while with my own thoughts about how I was feeling about my best friend and my favorite editor. My rational mind told me I was merely concerned that J.L. Kidston risked being unmasked, but it also wondered why Paul was in town without telling me that he was here. To the best of my knowledge, he had never actually come here before despite his company having a local office. I had not had any dealings with the local outpost at all. The non-rational side of me was seething with envy and what seemed to be a sense of rivalry which had never before existed between Isobel and me. And she was completely oblivious. It was very uncomfortable. I had only recently begun to wonder why I hadn't ever shared my whole story with my best friend. But there was just something delicious about having a secret. I took out my tablet to keep my mind off the whole distressing situation.

The athletes, then the artists...they all had their temptations, Olivia was thinking as her stilettos clicked determinedly across the marble floor of the foyer. But the research must continue. The hotel seemed to be filled with convention-goers, or so it seemed. She smoothed the lapel of her Chanel jacket and stopped briefly before a large poster proclaiming this an international convention of cosmetic surgeons. She licked her lips seductively (she could do it no other way) and noticed a tall, dark man with an endearing flick of curly hair flopping in his eyes slouching against the gilt-edged banister staring at her. She stared back. He licked his lower lip and thrust his hand deeper into his pocket. She moved slightly away from the poster, but could not seem to turn away from him. This was not good, she was thinking. I'm supposed to be in charge. But he had some kind of a hold on her. Olivia's breathing was suddenly rapid and shallow. That all too familiar feeling was making its way up her thighs and inward. Doctors, she thought briefly, were not on the list...

EIGHT

My literary musings were abruptly halted when I lifted my eyes from the screen for just a moment and caught sight of David Rubenstein passing by the window. As I may have mentioned in passing, one of the things I liked about this particular restaurant was that it was in a part of town where I was unlikely to ever see a single one of Eric's friends or colleagues.

I watched as he moved past the building and had to fight off the urge to follow him to see where he was going and even more interestingly, who he might be meeting in this part of town. Instead, I patted my lips with the paper napkin and paid my bill. The usual welcome relief of the early evening coolness was not evident today. I did a quick time check to find that it was just past 6:30, and although I really did not have a lot of time to meander around before my presences was required, I decided to browse one of my favorite haunts in the neighborhood: the local news stand. Like any magazine junkie worth her salt, I was drawn to newsstands wherever I went and this one was like a siren call for me. They carried over 2000 periodicals according to their sign in the window and for me it was like dying and going to heaven.

Sadly, though, I noticed that the 2000 was written over a 3500 that had been crossed out – a sign of the times, I could only guess. These days I had a kind of wistful feeling as I picked up a real magazine and held it in my hand. Given the rush to e-publication, I was thinking, it might not be too long before these were all collectors' items. The thought made me want to buy up the entire store!

The indulgent owners permitted browsing within the magazines before buying, a small kindness I had always appreciated. I was deep into the masthead of what was a new magazine to me when I heard a familiar laugh and an unfamiliar male voice that was close to a whisper. Peering over the top of the rack, I caught sight of David's mop of curly brown hair. I was surprised to see him in this kind of a shop, but then lots of people still read real newspapers, although there were lots of newspaper stands closer to his downtown office. I put the magazine I was browsing through back on the rack and walked around to the other side to say hello, but just as I was about to open my mouth, I noticed something peculiar. David and another man were standing side-by-side talking with a tall, blonde man who was sporting tortoise-shell glasses and a bright scarf knotted loosely around his neck in that European way that always looks so cool. The man beside David was shorter than he was and seemed to have his arm around David's waist in a

120

most intimate fashion. I backed away, puzzled by this odd threesome.

"David, I haven't seen you down here for ages. You look wonderful," the tall blonde said.

"Thanks. Yeah, it's been a while, but Sandy convinced me that we should pick up where we left off." He and 'Sandy' exchanged knowing glances.

I realized that I was eavesdropping, and worse, I was skulking. I felt a bit like those lurkers on Facebook, but this was for real; I couldn't tear myself away.

"We've all certainly missed David's sense of humor," Sandy said.

Sense of humor, I thought. I had known David for years and not once would I have ever described him as someone with a sense of humor. In fact, humorless was the descriptor that I'm fairly sure I'd used when discussing his demeanor with Isobel.

"Are you still taking new patients, David? I have a friend who could use a sympathetic doctor," said the blonde.

"Any friend of yours who needs a doctor is welcome in my office. Just tell him to get his doctor to send a referral and include his email address. I'll be glad to help if I can."

They said their good-byes then David and his friend left together. Although Sandy no longer had his arm around David's waist, there was something proprietary about the way he held the door for David, and then placed his hand fleetingly on his back.   I seemed to be having a lot of strange moments today. Perhaps I wasn't the only one with a secret.

I wandered around the shop for just a bit longer – I certainly didn't want to run into David on the street at this point. I stopped in front of the rack where David and Sandy had been standing noting that it was a rack of sailing magazines. I should have guessed: David was the proud owner of a 50-foot *Jeanneau*, a very expensive, hugely fancy sailboat about which I knew nothing except that Rebecca complained bitterly when he spent money she had earmarked for a very expensive holiday to the South Pacific. She did, however, subsequently take to the sailing life very quickly, making sure she had the latest in sailing gear and fashion. In fact, she often liked to talk about the boat at parties.

Sailing is one of those pastimes that are cultures onto themselves – a subculture of Yuppie life, but encompassing a host of others who have that affinity for wind and water.   Pictures in magazines of an impeccable white boat slipping silently through the tranquil, turquoise waters between Caribbean islands, usually the Virgin Islands, populated by tanned, lean sailor-types in pristine white sailing shorts and Sperry Top-Siders sipping margaritas at sunset are all lies. Lies, lies, lies.

Being a bona fide sailor means cold spring weekends spent on cleaning and upkeep, working your fingers to the bone, wearing dirty coveralls and spending every spare cent on equipment, maintenance, haul-up in the winter, storage, not to mention provisions for the ceaseless weekend guests. After all, if you keep it to yourself, who will ever know about the many amenities of your breathtakingly expensive toy? And everyone needs crew. Friends who have been plied with food and drink make the best crew, it seems, or at least the most guilt-ridden crew.

And those provisions are not likely to consist of hot dogs and beer – As I said, never beer for a Yuppie. No, it is more likely to be caviar, expensive French cheese and champagne if you happen to be married to Rebecca Rubenstein, she of the classic boating convert ilk. But you must never let your friends and acquaintances know the real truth about boating – that it is any different than the carefree lifestyle portrayed in those boating magazines. Unless, of course, they happen upon you up to your armpits in grease, as Eric and I did one cold, spring Saturday afternoon. As a result, Both David and especially Rebecca felt it necessary to restore our faith in the wonders of sailing by taking us out for a leisurely sail in their now pristine craft.

~

So this is how I found myself one sunny June morning setting out for the marina, wine in hand to meet David and Rebecca for a bracing day on the mighty Lake Ontario. I cannot say that I was completely in favor of the outing. I mean, to anyone who fears more than three feet of water, and who would be tempted to wear a life jacket in the bathtub, sailing is not exactly the most relaxing way to spend the day. But I am nothing if not a good sport. So that is how I ended up on David Rubenstein's boat for one of the most terrifying experiences of my life.

At the appointed time, Eric and I met David and Rebecca on the dock where the 'Gone with the Wind' (I kid you not, that was his boat's name – Rebecca's brainchild) was tethered. I know that's probably not the right word – but I'm not one of those boat people. It was truly magnificent. Fifty feet from bow to stern (impressed?), it was pristine white fibreglass and boasted two cabins – one with a king-sized bed – a full bathroom and more burl wood than I'd ever seen in my life. It was everywhere. It had a single, enormous mast.

The sails were rolled up and enclosed in blue canvas coverings. Attached to the mast was a confusing array of ropes and pulleys: I had no idea
124

what they were for, but they did seem important. I
began at that moment to develop a kind of grudging
respect for David. Anyone who had the ability to
unravel those ropes and make them do something
useful had my everlasting admiration. Even more
impressive was that David seemed to actually enjoy
this task. But I supposed it was really the sort of
thing he did every day, unravelling people's urinary
systems in the operating room.

David and Rebecca were the poster children for
the 'boat people.' Of all the sports Eric introduced
me to over the course of our marriage, I think that
the one I coveted the most was the life of the
seasoned sailor. Perhaps it was because I actually
feared it. I never learned to swim, yet have a great
fascination with the ocean – a very large lake would
be a good stand-in, though. The last time I had
taken swimming lessons was after a trip to the
Bahamas wherein I nearly drowned. However, after
nearly losing my swimsuit during the first lesson at
the YWCA (my swimsuits were actually misnamed,
being more for sun than swim), I decided that if
God had wanted human beings to live in the water
instead of beside it, she would have given us gills,
so I gave up the pursuit.

Anyway, David was kitted out in a white and
navy striped polo shirt, pristine white pants and the
inevitable Sperry's just like in the movies. He cut a

dashing figure, and in my mind's eye I could see Humphrey Bogart leaning against the mast languidly smoking a cigarette. Very romantic. Rebecca was similarly sailor-attired. My admiration for my friends soared.

"Come aboard," David said, after hopping with some agility from the dock onto the boat deck. David, being rather short and just slightly portly (not really the image of Bogie – that was all in my mind), was actually in far better shape than I had ever given him credit for. Rebecca, on the other hand, was the picture of the fit woman, a testimony to the hours she spent in the gym perfecting her "delts" and sweating through class after class of hot yoga that was trending among the Yuppies. Slightly taller than her husband, she had also spent many hours perfecting her tennis and squash technique, and naturally, she skied. However, as I watched Rebecca go aboard in front of me, I got the distinct impression that she was a bit of a fish out of water, so to speak. There was a slightly palpable sense of unease.

As Eric and I got aboard I was thinking that he was especially looking forward to this day since he was hoping for a sailing lesson of sorts from David. For the past week he had been pouring over a book filled with photos and drawings of boats, ropes, masts, sails and everything associated with the sport. He had the terminology down – I did not.

126

Within five minutes of getting aboard and stowing our bags, we had drinks in our hands – champagne to be exact. That is all of us except David had drinks. One of his cardinal rules of sailing evidently was that under no circumstances was the skipper permitted to drink. I felt that this was a wise decision and raised my glass accordingly.

The sun was shining brightly over the marina as we pulled away from the dock powered by the engine. Sitting on the deck with my head back to feel the warmth of the early season sun, I started to relax a bit and thought that I might just enjoy this sailing. I wasn't even wearing a life jacket, fool that I was, although it was in sight. After we left the shelter of the cove, the wind started to pick up. This invigorated both Eric and David who began hoisting the main sail. He started shouting instructions to both Rebecca and Eric both of whom followed his every word – most of which I failed to understand. I did, however, feel as if I ought to be doing something.

"Could I help?" I shouted to David over the wind which had really increased in velocity in just a few minutes.

"Why don't you go below and see to lunch? As soon as we get these sails set we'll settle in for a nice, smooth sail and a bit of sustenance."

127

This was right up my alley so I was happy to comply. I eased myself down the narrow steps into the galley below. Having very little experience with boats up to that moment, I had nothing with which to compare this one, but it did seem to me to be very nice. Everything was blue and white and teak and battened down. The kitchen seemed to have all the amenities of home, just in miniature or so it seemed.

I opened the containers of lobster and potato salad, the boat began to list to the right (starboard?). I had a moment of panic until I remembered Eric's instructions on the way over in the car. I was not to be concerned about this kind of movement because it would mean simply that the sails were taking the wind – or something to that effect. The boat then righted itself anyway and I reminded myself that this is what sailing is all about. I had seen boats at full sail and the often seemed to be listing to the side for reasons previously unknown to a non-sailor type like me. Truth be told, though, I did think that it looked a bit precarious.

I started humming to myself as I set out the plates. I was trying to get my sea legs under me as the gentle rocking seemed to be getting more pronounced. Suddenly I started to feel a bit queasy so decided that a bit of fresh air would do me good. I climbed back up the steps and opened the door to the deck only to be greeted by a blast of wind that
128

knocked me off balance causing me to tumble backwards down the stairs in a most undignified manner. I was starting to feel a bit scared that all was not well. We had now been out for just over an hour and the weather had changed dramatically. The sun was no longer shining and I was fairly certain that I had felt some sea spray with that blast of wind. I scrambled up to the table and found a life jacket that Rebecca had left on the seat. Once I had myself buckled in, I felt considerably safer and thought I'd brave the wind once again.

Just as I poked my head out the door, Eric screamed at me. "Go back down, Alex! You know you can't swim!"

Eric looked to be hanging onto a rope for dear life as if we might be going down. In an unexpected flash of clarity, it dawned on me that if that were in fact the case, it would be much safer to be outside on the deck with my life jacket on rather than being trapped inside, lack of swimming skills notwithstanding. Of course, what I did not know until Eric told me about it later, we were not going down at all. I stayed put on the deck anyway.

My sandals were not made for slippery, wet boat decks and the first step I took caused me to slide perilously across the deck finding myself jammed up against the very low, and to my mind unsafe, railing. I heard a blood-curdling scream and realized it had come from me. Terrified of drowning, my worst fear in life, I tried desperately to get myself back to the door to take my chances inside rather than face sure death by sliding overboard.

By now the rain that had only just begun to splash across the deck when I first came topside (a new word I had learned that morning), was gushing down and I was soaked. I finally made it to the door and slid down into the cabin. Paralyzed with fear, I sat on the floor and looked up at the portholes. As the boat listed, the water line actually covered the windows. Then, as quickly as the rocking had started, it stopped, and all was calm. I said a silent prayer and decided then and there that I would never set foot on a sail boat again regardless of the attraction of the lifestyle. And no matter what Eric said, I knew that his desire to learn how to sail meant that he'd eventually want his own boat. *Over my dead body*, I thought. Then took that back.

Rebecca made her way down the steps. "That was quite thrilling, don't you think, Alex?"

Who is she kidding? I thought. She had looked almost as terrified as I felt. And thrilling wasn't the word I would have used. "Does this sort of thing happen often?" I said through chattering teeth.

"David only wishes," she said as she began to clean up the mess that was our lunch by that time.
130

"He says that you can only really prove yourself as a sailor if nature challenges you. I do prefer calm-weather sailing, myself, though." She had put down the dishes she was cleaning up and had begun examining her nails. "Damn! I've broken a nail. And I've gotten my outfit dirty. I think I'll go and change," she said, making her way to the stateroom farther in. Won't be a minute."

I could scarcely believe her. Our lives had been in mortal danger only minutes ago and all she could think about were her clothes and her nails. So, what was I being a cry baby about? I had sat here on the floor while she had been outside presumably helping. Anyway, I decided the least I could do was to finish cleaning up and serve lunch.

By the time Rebecca had repaired her nails and her outfit, I had the plates heaped high with lobster, organic caviar and salmon mousse and was balancing a tray as I took the food up on deck – where the sun was shining again. She picked up another bottle of champagne and followed me.

Up on deck, David was showing Eric some intricacies of the ropes and explaining the features and benefits of this particular model. Dear god, was Eric really thinking about buying one of these death traps? I would never be a party to a hole in the water into which one poured money as the saying goes.

"Miss, are you going to buy that magazine or just make love to it?"

I came abruptly back to the present from my sailing daydream to find myself caressing a sailing magazine so earnestly that I was rubbing the print off the cover. I had blue ink all over my hands.

"Oh, I'm terribly sorry," I said. "Yes, I'm going to buy this."

Although they do let you read without buying, manhandling the merchandise is another matter. I paid for my unwanted purchase, glancing at my watch as I put the change back in my wallet. Yikes, it was getting late; Eric would probably be frantic as to my whereabouts. He was preternaturally punctual and I was expected to be the same. I did wonder, however, if today he'd notice in the state in which I left him. I only hoped he hadn't continued with his drink fest. This would go down in the annals of my life as one of the most peculiar days I could remember.

As I left the store, I walked into an olfactory assault of over-heated sewer mixed with diesel fuel from the bus that had just pulled away from the bus stop after disgorging what appeared to me to be an inordinately large number of people. I hurried through the crowd as quickly as the throng and the heat would permit. As I enclosed myself in my stifling little car, I lusted for a moment for air

132

conditioning, but the feeling passed quickly. The weather will change soon enough, I told myself.

I opened my window and moved out of the parking space into traffic, clicking the record app on my cell phone. I started talking.

Olivia was beginning to wonder what was happening. She had been drawn to the tall, slouching man like a moth is drawn to a flame; there was no doubt about the heat. She had readily agreed to meet him in the lobby later. She had taken a magnificent suite on the 39th floor – the one where "the Donald" himself stayed when in town. But he had other plans. She allowed herself to be led out of the hotel into the back of a waiting limousine where champagne was on ice and caviar sparkled in the silver dish alongside. She did not ask their destination. Fifteen minutes and two glasses of Moët & Chandon later the driver offered his hand to help her out of the car into the setting sun. Olivia adjusted her D & G sunglasses and took in the private entrance to the marina. As she and the man walked arm in arm down the jetty toward a magnificent yacht she breathed in the setting sun in all its crimson glory reflected in the calm waters of the bay. It was, after all, going to be perfect, she was thinking. Just then she spotted a slim figure standing by the mast on the deck of the

133

waiting boat. As they moved closer, she could finally make out that it was a woman. A perfect woman wearing the lower half of a bikini. She was momentarily puzzled. He squeezed her arm into himself and asked her if she minded if they were joined by his wife. Olivia shuddered just a bit, and then a small smile began playing around her mouth. This was not in my plans, she was thinking, but, as she looked more closely at the woman who was now embracing the man Olivia began to think that abandoning her carefully crafted plan for one evening couldn't possibly derail everything. By now the man was arranging pillows on the deck as the crew materialized out of nowhere. He asked Olivia if she would like to make herself more comfortable and handed her the bottom half of a string bikini. Olivia smiled.

NINE

Eric was only partially ready for the party when I arrived home. I had half expected to see him fully clothed and pacing up and down our living room, periodically looking at his Rolex, muttering about me being late, which was what he usually did in these situations. Instead, I found him drink in hand, lying on our bed with his shirt and tie on and nothing else. Absolutely nothing. At least he was holding a glass of wine now rather than a beer. Perhaps all was right with the world once again.

"Did you and Isobel enjoy another of your deep, intellectual conversations?"

I must say that I have never found sarcasm becoming in a man. Though it may be catty in a woman, it is thoroughly odious in a man. He was a master.

I didn't dignify this with an answer, rather looked around since things still seemed to be a bit out of whack. Beside him on the bed was a pile of books. At first glance I thought that he might be researching something (which may have been true), but what he was researching was beyond me. I walked over to pick up the book on the top of the pile. It was one of my writing reference guides. Given my stock in trade, it was representative of the many books I had on corporate writing. To my great relief it wasn't anything like "How to Write Erotic Novels." It was William Zinsser's "On Writing Well", a classic I often recommended to our interns at the office. Under that one were three of four more books, novels all, each of them in a different genre, and each belonging to me. I was a sort of promiscuous reader, never sticking to one writer or even genre for long.

"What are you doing with my books?"

"Just getting to know my wife better," he said taking a sip from the crystal wine goblet he was holding by the stem. At all times he was the wine connoisseur extraordinaire. At least he had moved back to wine, a more familiar drug of choice in his world.

"Most of these books are really old," I said. "They've been around the house almost as long as we've been married. Why the sudden interest in my reading habits?"

"Well, today is our tenth wedding anniversary, and I'm feeling a bit nostalgic, as it were. I was thinking that there were no surprises any more. But just when I thought that, well, you never know what you might find out about your spouse. Never a dull moment."

Never a dull moment? Was he talking about us? Where in the world did he get an idea like that?

136

"Eric, I think that you've had altogether too much to drink this evening already. I think you're beginning to lose your grip on reality."

"And not a moment too soon, my darling. Not a moment too soon." He began sniffing the armpits of his shirt. "Awfully warm today, don't you think?"

"I'm going to get dressed. I suggest you do the same," I said as I turned toward the bathroom removing articles of clothing as I went. I'd had just about enough of this ridiculous conversation that seemed to be going nowhere fast. I couldn't for a moment fathom what he was on about. What new things did he think he knew about me? I, on the other hand, figured I knew just about everything I wanted to know about the man I had thought I'd loved so much those ten, long years ago. Indeed, this was a new side of my husband that I had not seen before, and I didn't like it any more than I liked the old side. I turned back to tell Eric to hurry up and get dressed, and just as I was about to close the door to the ensuite bathroom, I noticed a book sticking out from under the bed skirt. I could see only a small corner of the cover, but it was all I needed. The cover was gray, and I didn't need to see any more than that corner to know that there were 50 shades of it between that front cover and the back. Now, I got it. Dear god, he thought I was a rabid fan of women's erotica. Just what was he expecting lying there without his pants on, anyway? I took a deep breath and closed the door behind me. I only hoped that he'd be ready to roll when I finished my shower.

A half an hour later when I emerged from the bathroom, he was nowhere to be found. As I was opening the closet to find the dress I'd set aside for this evening, I happened to glance at the sort of rogues' gallery of photos that I kept on my dresser. There were six framed photos each depicting an important milestone in my recent life. Alongside the picture of my parents was a sterling silver-framed wedding picture of Eric and me. There I was, ten years ago, looking a lifetime younger, smiling at the world, without a clue about what life had in store for me. Clueless. The word lingered in my mind for a moment until the photo in front of it caught my attention. It was of Isobel and me taken five years ago in Vegas, and well, you know what they say about the things that go on in Vegas.

~

It all started one winter when the winter started to get the better of me, and yearning for a palm tree, I tried to cajole Eric into jetting away with me for a week – just a week, I promised. He simply could not get away, he said. Too many patients, he said. The excuses were the usual ones: I'll lose too much money, what will my patients do without me etc.
138

I'd had enough. I refused to coax him this time. So, I remember saying to him, fine. Stay in your office. It won't stop me, though. And it didn't.

I called Isobel and asked her what she intended to do with her upcoming winter vacation break. Club Med, was her thinking, although she hadn't made any plans at that point. I began to have fantasies about the two of us on a Club Med beach and then snapped back to reality: I was married. There would be expectations that I couldn't fulfil. There would be just too many compromising situations if I read the online reviews and brochures correctly. So we decided to go to Vegas for five days. The day I arrived home, tickets in hand, Eric decided that perhaps he wasn't so busy after all. Perhaps he'd like to come. It was too late, I told him. It was going to be a girlfriends' vacation.

Eric spent the next three weeks before our departure date trying to talk me out of going. He told me he had heard all sorts of stories about Vegas, and that I would most certainly not be safe. All of his needling just made me more anxious to get away. Besides, I told him, we were simply going to get some sun, see a couple of shows and do some serious shopping. Maybe we'd even take a few tennis lessons. God knows, my tennis could use improvement. He couldn't disagree with that argument.

We left in the middle of a February snow storm, almost not making the plane because of treacherous road conditions. It was a wonder that the planes were flying, but except for a few delays, all systems were a go. So Isobel and I boarded the plane, had several glasses of wine and were well on our way.

As our plane banked and made its way toward the runway, I was amazed by the sight below us: it seemed that we might just land right on "the strip", that was how close the runway was to the street, or so it seemed from our vantage point. From the moment we stepped into the airport we knew that we were not "in Kansas" anymore. We weren't even in Toronto.

As we made our way through the departure lounge to the baggage carousel, it became clear to us that gambling was the heart and soul of this place. Duh! It wasn't' really on our radar, but as we watched the departing passengers putting one last coin into the slot machines that lines the walls, we began to think that we might just try it.

We were booked into the Venetian, right on the strip. It seemed just campy enough for the two of us to feel we had gotten away completely. As our taxi pulled up in front of the hotel I felt like I was in Disney Land for adults. We turned in past the tower of St. Mark's church and a Venetian bridge.

140

We clambered out of the cab and into a magnificent lobby.

"Are we in the right place?" I wondered aloud. "I mean, how much is this costing us?"

"Alex, that's the beauty of Las Vegas. Everything is over the top, even the cheap accommodations."

That was something of an understatement. We were booked into their cheapest accommodation: a double-king-bedded suite. Yes, a suite. The place has 3000 suites of varying sizes and costs, and it occurred to me that couldn't be a bad one in the place. We were on the 28th floor and had a wonderful view of the strip – I think we were slightly upgraded, based on the view which could possibly have been out the back.

The huge bathroom had double sinks, marble-looking walls and a 17-inch television! It occurred to me that I might never leave – but leave we did. Almost immediately, or at least after a brief discussion of our options. Explore the strip? Find a bar? Go to the pool? Since we had left in a snow storm, it seemed appropriate to find a pool with a bar and leave the strip until later. We donned bikinis, cover-ups, platform sandals, over-sized sunglasses and floppy-brimmed straw hats that we had squished into our luggage at the last minute and were off.

Isobel had kind of a homing device for bars, but this time she didn't need it. We had just settled on a couple of loungers when a cocktail waitress asked us if she could help. Indeed, she could. Rather than the martinis that we loved, we decided on champagne to celebrate the sun and our escape. A few minutes later, the smiling cocktail waitress with the longest, most perfectly tanned legs I'd ever seen, returned with two flutes on a silver tray. She placed the drinks on the little tables beside the loungers and we watched the bubbles envelop the perfectly shaped strawberry in the bottom of each of the glasses. We were truly in heaven.

I took a deep breath of the warm air, a sip of the bubbly and lay back on the lounger, closing my eyes. Isobel, on the other hand, was wired. She sat up sipping her champagne and eyeballing the guests.

"Alex."

I didn't move.

"Alex, are you asleep?"

I opened an eye behind my over-sized shades. "Not yet. What's up?"

"Do you see those two guys over there?"

I looked in the direction that she was nodding. All I could see was two older men upon whom I would not have bestowed the moniker "guys." They looked like someone's fathers.

"I think the one in the Ray-ban Wayfarers is interested."

"Interested in what?" I said, lying back down.

"Me," she said. "I mean us."

"Isobel, first, may I remind you that I'm married and strictly off-limits. And second, we are here for a girlfriends' get-away."

"Yes, of course, I know all that. But it can't hurt to look, can it?"

"Whatever, but couldn't you at least pick a couple of guys worth ogling?" I peeked at her over my sunglasses to find her studying the two men in question.

"I think they're cute. I'm going over to say hello."

I sighed. Isobel was clearly planning to do more than sightsee and shop. I supposed that I couldn't blame her, though. She wasn't the one trying to escape from her husband for a few days. Oops, I meant escape winter.

The next day Isobel had a dilemma. "Alex," she began as we unloaded the spoils of our shopping spree onto the two king-sized beds in our room. "Alex, I was wondering if you might spend a few hours with Hans this evening."

Why on earth would I do that, I wondered. "Why on earth would I do that, Isobel?"

"Well, so you won't be alone. I'd love to have a few hours with Jürgen."

Hans and Jürgen were the two men by the pool in the speedos. Of course, I had immediately drawn the conclusion that they were Europeans and I was entirely correct. Hailing from Switzerland, they were in Vegas to attend the gargantuan technology conference that was going on at the hotel. The place was crawling with both geeky types and sales types. I concluded that they were the latter.

"Isobel, I can stay by myself. I don't need to spend a few hours with anyone."

"But you'll stay in our room and watch movies, won't you?"

I shrugged.

"Well, that's just not right. You can't waste an evening in Vegas. So, it's settled. You'll have dinner with Hans."

I couldn't help rolling my eyes.

Anyway, the evening went according to Isobel's pan. She spent the evening with Jürgen, and I met Hans for dinner. As we walked along the strip toward the MGM Grand where we had dinner reservations, he pulled out his pack of cigarettes. "You don't mind if I smoke?" It was more of a statement than a question.

As a matter of fact I did mind, but I didn't want to appear rude, so he lit up. He was smoking those vile cigarettes that one can buy only in Europe. I

144

started to cough – but only slightly. I knew that I was being passive-aggressive, but I couldn't help myself. I know I should have been more assertive and just told him that I most certainly did mind. The coughing, it has to be said, had absolutely no effect on him. So I coughed louder. By the time he got the message, we had arrived at the hotel and he was forced to put it out anyway. But the scent lingered – all evening.

The evening dragged on as we discovered that we had nothing whatsoever in common. He was interested in all things technological and comics; I was not. At first I thought that I might get some really good tech tips from him, but it seemed that his interests ran more to "Assassin's Creed" and "Marvel Heroes" than to smartphone apps and eBooks. I started to miss Eric.

~

My cell phone pinged with the 30 minute warning that we were expected as guests at our own anniversary party – and I was immediately jolted back to the present reality.

I picked up the photo of Isobel and me, smiling as we posed on one of the fake Venetian bridges that connect up all parts of the Venetian resort. Jürgen had taken the photo on our last day in Vegas. So fake, I thought, and then looked around at my bedroom. So fake, I thought.

I wondered if it would have been the same if we had actually gone to Venice – the real Venice – if we had walked through Piazza San Marco, across the Bridge of Sighs, along the Guidecca canal – if it had been more real. Perhaps we could do that some time. But right now, I had to play nice.

TEN

"Perhaps you'd better drive tonight, Alex," Eric said handing me his car keys when I found him in the living room fully clothed at last. "I believe I may have had a drink or two."

Much to my surprise, regardless of the number of drinks he had imbibed, Eric was immaculate as usual.

"Of course. But I don't need your keys. I have my own," I said pulling them out of the depths of my favorite Mulberry bag and waving them in front of him.

Eric clutched his heart dramatically. "Good god, Alex, you don't think I'm so drunk that I would consent to arriving at David and Rebecca's party in your old clunker?"

He never gave up, drunk or sober.

I knew that there was no point in pursuing the matter any further; it was akin to arguing with a two-year old in these matters. I took the keys to his pride and joy, slid my purse over my elbow without another word and headed to the car.

As we got into the car that was parked in front of the house (the driveway was in the back behind the row of town houses), I saw our neighbors emerge into their puny front yard with their two children in tow. They seemed to be dressed for some kind of fancy party. They waved and I remembered that Judith, the mom, had told me they were preparing for their oldest daughter's Bat Mitzvah. There seemed to be a lot of dress-up occasions leading up to it. As I pulled the car away from the curb, I remembered that it was a similar kind of event where I met David and Rebecca for the first time.

~

Being brought up as a good Catholic girl in a small town, I had never even been inside a Baptist church until my friends started getting married when I was in my early 20's. I had certainly never had the occasion to experience a synagogue – I think that there may have been two Jewish families in my home town. Maybe. Diverse it was not.

Isobel and I had often laughed about this, but she had never been inside a Catholic Church until my wedding to Eric ten years ago. At least there was one benefit of our longstanding friendship: we broadened one another's cultural horizons. To mitigate my ignorance, Isobel had decided that I should attend her cousin's Bat Mitzvah with her. She told me that it would be the ideal occasion in which to be initiated into one of the parts of her life that I didn't understand. So, she wrangled an invitation, I dressed up as instructed, and we were off to the synagogue one sunny June Saturday morning.

Trying to put this religious occasion into context with what I was familiar with in my own life, after Isobel explained it to me, I concluded that it was similar to what I understood about confirmation. I figured that there would be a religious ceremony for a dozen or two young people after which we would adjourn to the church (or in this case synagogue) hall for refreshments. After that, I expected that we would watch as all of the new initiates had their photos taken on the lawn with their parents, and then we would go home. Perhaps several privileged guests would be invited back home for a drink. That is what I expected. I was so wrong.

First, Isobel's cousin Susan was one of only two young women taking part in the ceremony that day. When I entered the synagogue, it occurred to me that it looked much more like a church than I expected. However, it was much more luxurious. As we sat down, the familiarity of the surroundings made me start to relax a bit. I watched as the rest of the congregation began to make their way to their seats, and Isobel began to give me a running commentary.

"You see that woman in the wild purple dress and brimmed hat?" she asked.

I did see her, but I was becoming concerned that we perhaps ought not to be whispering and talking so much.

"That's Aunt Myra. She's my cousin Rebecca's mother. You know, I've told you about her."

I had never met Rebecca, but had heard a lot about her. She was not one of Isobel's favorite people.

"Isobel," I whispered as quietly as I could, hoping she might follow my lead, "don't you think we ought to be quiet?"

Isobel's eyes widened in surprise. "Whatever for?" She looked at me and started to laugh. "You do have a lot to learn about other people's religious behavior, don't you?" She snorted loudly.

I looked around to see if anyone had noticed. They did not seem to have. In fact, it seemed that everyone around us was engaged in rather louder conversations that I had ever before heard in a place of worship. As more and more seats filled, the din became even more concentrated. Then the ceremony began, and there was quiet. For a little while.

I was utterly transfixed. These two young, Jewish women being formally ushered into the ranks of the adult women of their community had obviously spent years preparing for this event. They had learned Hebrew, and by my own
150

estimation, seemed to be among the only people in the room who still knew what it all meant. Everyone else was following along with the English translation, at least before striking up a new conversation with someone in front of them, beside them, or behind them. And when that conversation grew tiresome, they just got up to go across the aisle to begin another one with someone fresh. In the midst of all this, there were two tiny, dark-haired children crawling up the aisle toward the Rabbi while their fathers stood in the aisle, arms folded, talking and clearly oblivious to their wandering offspring.

Even if they were not so engrossed, I was riveted to the proceedings. It was as foreign to me as the Hebrew words on the pages in front of me that were being read right to left instead of left to right. I began to realize that for Isobel and her family, being Jewish was so much more than simply following the tenets of a religion – it was a culture.

When the ceremony was over an hour later, Isobel told me that I was lucky to have been at a Bat Mitzvah rather than a Bar Mitzvah for my first synagogue experience since according to her, they usually lasted three hours! We made our way downstairs to the hall that had already been prepared for the arrival of a horde of hungry people. As we entered the reception in the crush of people, I caught sight of long lines of tables groaning under the weight of massive amounts of food and drink. I was only able to get a brief glimpse, however, before they were surrounded by seemingly ravenous hordes. I had never seen anything like it: within moments, everyone seemed to be chewing in unison.

I must have looked slightly alarmed, because when Isobel looked over, she laughed and put her arm around my shoulders, leading me toward the bar. She immediately had two glasses of kosher wine and was pressing one into my willing hand.

"I want to introduce you to my Aunt Myra," she said, steering me though the crowd. "She's such a character; I think you'll love her. Her husband died two years ago, and she's been scandalizing the family ever since with her trips around the world and her insistence that there was no need to confine her dating to nice, older Jewish widowers – preferably rich ones if her daughters had their way. "

When Aunt Myra caught sight of Isobel, she turned abruptly away from whomever she was conversing with and made her way to meet us half-way. It was clear that Aunt Myra was fond of her niece.

"Izzy," she said, "you're a breath of fresh air in this crowd of hot gas!"

I had never heard anyone refer to Isobel as Izzy; in fact, Isobel had told me once in no uncertain terms that she was not a nickname kind of gal. I smiled. I knew that I was going to like this eccentric woman who was now taking Isobel's face between her two hands and kissing her on both cheeks. Then she immediately turned her attention to me.

"And you, my dear, must be Alex! I've heard so much about you over the past few years from our Izzy, but she didn't mention how very pretty you are. Welcome to the family!"

And with that she took my face between her two hands and planted kisses on each side of my face. Aunt Myra then began chattering rapidly to Isobel about this and that person, all the while making her way through the crowd that seemed to part to let her through toward the buffet table. She continued talking as she heaped a plate with food, and then continued as she began to eat. Between sentences she popped pieces of smoked salmon into her mouth; they seemed to disappear in the time it took her to take a breath. That was the first time I had ever seen anyone really and truly inhale her food!

Isobel decided that in an attempt to give me a more balanced view of what I was beginning to think was a seriously fun family, I would have to meet Myra's daughter, Rebecca. She waved good-bye to Aunt Myra and steered me toward the dessert table which seemed to be surrounded by a slightly younger knot of people. I noticed that they were all dressed in the very latest of elegant fashion, and they seemed to have a curious way of eyeing each other kind of sideways as they talked. It almost seemed as if they were all a bit on their guard. I was sure I saw Isobel's nose start to twitch as we neared the exclusive little group.

"Rebecca," she said as we closed in on them.

The most elegant of the bunch turned toward Isobel and quickly sized us both up.

"Rebecca, I'd like you to meet my friend Alex." Isobel then turned toward a short man with curly, black hair. "And Alex, this is David, Rebecca's husband."

"I'm so pleased to meet both of you," I said, extending my hand toward Rebecca who pretended not to notice it. David shook it instead.

"It's always nice to see a fresh face at these gatherings," David said. He seemed about to say something else when an urgent bleating began emanating from somewhere in the vicinity of his belt.

"That sounds like the hospital, darling," Rebecca drawled. "They must need you." Rebecca now turned toward me. "David is a urology resident, you know. They just cannot seem to get along without him even for a few hours."

David didn't look nearly as pleased at the interruption of his off-hours as did his wife, but he excused himself to take the call. He would need somewhere considerably quieter to even hear what was being said on the other end of a cell phone – that would probably be about three blocks away in my estimation.

"You can't blame a person for her relatives," Isobel was saying as we headed back to the bar for a refill.

~

Eric and I were now driving along the street where Rebecca and the hapless David now lived. They had come a long way from his residency. The houses were impressive to say the least; I could remember when the trees lining the leafy street had been mere saplings when they first moved in and we'd been invited to the house warming party. We'd become a fixture in their social circle since I first met them, much to Eric's delight. Time really did fly by.

Rebecca had been a Yuppie-by-marriage. Unwilling (or unable – I was never sure of the details) to finish college, she had worked for a couple of years as a receptionist at a fashion magazine. I always pictured her schlepping coffee to a devil-wears-Prada kind of boss lady, but she didn't like to talk about her life before David. They had been high school sweet hearts, but according to Isobel she had not so much as given him the time of day back then. It seemed his acceptance to medical school had changed her attitude toward the nerdy short guy. After he had finished his residency, found a position as a staff urologist, and started to earn serious money, Rebecca had embraced the Yuppie lifestyle with the fervor of any religious convert. Her behavior often reminded me that my mother had been known to opine that converts made the best Catholics – Rebecca was the most devout Yuppie that I knew. Next to Eric, that is.

She was as devoted to her chosen lifestyle as if she had been born with a vocation. He had her requisite two children on whom she lavished everything: private schools, private music lessons, private hockey coaching, private parties, private, private, private. Considering how utterly enamoured she was of the notion of privacy, it seemed almost obscene the way she talked incessantly about them and their accomplishments – as dubious as some of them sounded.

Rebecca played racquetball almost daily – a bit of an homage to the Yuppies of the 1980's, I always thought. Then she had embraced the latest fad – hot yoga – with such zeal it was almost frightening. Always the epitome of the perfect wife, Rebecca had never made a single meaningful, independent statement in her life at least within earshot of me. Obviously she had no idea what David might be doing on all those very long nights at the hospital when he was supposedly crushing kidney stones with a lithotripsy machine.

Rebecca was inordinately fond of new things. I was remembering her yard sale when I was lovingly coveting a pair of silver candle sticks and a matching bon-bon dish. (It was the only time in my life when I was trying to become the perfect hostess. Luckily, the malaise passed.). When I asked her why she wanted to part with such beautiful objects, she told me that they didn't fit her lifestyle any longer. In fact, she had gone on to tell me that the cardinal rule of any good yard sale was to be sure to sell a few really special things so that the neighbors didn't get the 'wrong' impression. When I confided this newly acquired piece of information to Isobel later, she told me that what Rebecca really should have said was that her neighbors were such snobs, she just wanted them to be assured she was one of them. I shook my head, and yet I almost understood her. Then Isobel told me that when she'd gone over to help set up for the yard sale, Rebecca had gone into the house at one point and returned with a painting that hung over the fireplace in the dining room. It was a painting

157

that, by all accounts, Rebecca loved. When she was asked about it, she was reported to have said, "Oh, I don't expect anyone to buy it. I just wanted to attract the right sort of people."

A few days after the yard sale, Isobel and I were having lunch.

"You should have been there when David came home and noticed that the painting was missing."

"Go on," I said.

"I had just poured Rebecca her third glass of wine when he came into the den and asked if she had sent the painting out to be reframed again."

"Wasn't it back in the dining room by that time?"

Isobel laughed. "Not exactly. At least not Rebecca's. She sold it. When she told David, I thought he'd burst an artery. He started to turn purple so I thought I should leave."

I remembered that we could barely stop laughing.

~

As I opened the car door to step outside, I noticed that Eric was asleep in the passenger seat, embraced by the clutch of the Italian leather of his car's upholstery. I closed the door again, turned on the air conditioner again, got out my pen and notebook, and let him have another ten minutes. It was going to be a long evening as it was.

Olivia was back in New York – and that was just the way she wanted it. She loved the frisson of the city; it had a magic that always made her feel more alive. But as she sank back into the Italian leather seat in the back of the limousine, she was feeling a bit out of sorts. She had not yet accomplished what she had set out to do and she was now closing in on her penthouse. She simply wasn't ready. She had been searching for something that she had still not found. She had been sampling the buffet and was still hungry. She absently sipped the champagne that her driver had opened for her just before she stepped into the welcoming interior of her familiar car at the airport. She was thinking about the evening ahead. After a stop-off at the penthouse, her driver would return to take her to a party. She sighed to herself. It would be the same people, having the same conversations, sipping the same cocktails. Surely something different could happen tonight? After all, she had to be just a little different from when she left on her journey. She took another sip.

PART 2

"THE PLEASURE OF YOUR COMPANY IS REQUESTED…"

"There are no secrets better kept than the secrets that everybody guesses."
- George Bernard Shaw, "Mrs. Warren's Profession," 1893

ELEVEN

The purpose of a party is not what you might think. For many otherwise "normal" people the purpose of this particular party would probably be to wish dear friends a happy tenth anniversary and give them good wishes for many more. Not so much in the world of the Yuppies. No, the purpose of this or any other Yuppie party is to impress as many people as rapidly as you can. At least that is the host and hostess's purpose. The purpose of any party for everyone else is to "network", a quaint concept carried over from the first Yuppie wave in the 80's.

I cannot imagine that there is anyone who is unfamiliar with the term, but just in case, networking is the utilization of myriad communication skills to enhance and strengthen one's personal and professional power base by establishing previously unavailable relationships and reinforcing those which have been judged to be serviceable. Or you could just say that it's talking to (and more importantly if you can manage it) listening to people whom you judge to be useful, and ignoring others who won't help to raise your social or professional status. So tiresome!

161

Being the host or hostess of such a gathering is a bit like playing blackjack: there is a bit of strategy, but in the end it's really all about luck. You're destined to win big, or lose it all – if you let your gambling get out of hand. Either way, it enhances what Yuppies-at-work like to call your "social capital."

Rebecca Rubenstein, it needs to be said, was never much of a gambler, unless she thought she had a sure thing. She could be relied upon to leave little to chance and tonight would be no exception. The idea was to make the party and all its accoutrements look absolutely effortless, despite the fact that it had taken no fewer than two months to plan the menu, a full day to negotiate with the caterer (I did mention that Rebecca's major talent was hiring help, didn't I?), two florists' assistants to provide the understated and tasteful, but obviously expensive, décor, two rent-a-maids as well as the weekly cleaning lady to make sure that even the door frames could pass the white-glove test (don't kid yourself, at least one guest would be likely to surreptitiously run a finger across those pesky and hard-to-reach spots), and of course the caterer's chef, two servers and a bar tender to round out the personnel for the low-key evening. These occasions were nothing to sneeze at and I was somewhat chastened to think that I'd had ever had a derisive word to say about Rebecca because this

162

was all to celebrate the occasion of Eric's and my anniversary. Except, as you can probably tell, it really wasn't. In any case, a week or two later Dr. Rubenstein himself would get the bills and have an apoplectic seizure since Mrs. Rubenstein had probably grossly underestimated the bottom line. At least that had happened several times before.

Eric roused himself from his drunken stupor, checked his teeth and hair in the mirror, pulled out a piece of dental floss for a quickie and joined me as we made our way down the street toward the grand pile that the Rubenstein's called home.

"Darlings, how lovely to see you," Rebecca said as with a certain flourish she gestured to us to come in. "Everyone!" she called into the house, "the guests of honor are here!"

As usual, she was impeccably dressed in an oxblood cocktail dress with a bejewelled, draping neckline that didn't quite conceal the fact that she had recently been released from the clinic where she occasionally checked herself in to have her recurring anorexia treated. She was painfully thin, her collar bones clearly visible protrusions from her décolletage. She had told me she only attended the clinic to humor David whom she thought liked plumper women. Oh, how wrong we can be! I remember her telling me that she subscribed to the Wallis Simpson, the Duchess of Windsor's famous

163

motto: "You can never be too rich or too thin." Then she added her new favorite line, "Nothing tastes as good as being thin feels!"

She turned her attention back to us. "I did hope my guests of honor would be a bit earlier," she said pouting. "But better late than never."

"Thank-you so much for hosting this party for us," Eric said, smoothing his hair and then embracing her with more fervour than I had seen him exhibit of late.

Of course it had to be the alcohol that was now coursing through his veins, but Rebecca, clearly overwhelmed and responsive to his embrace, must have thought that he was simply enthralled by her beauty and charm.

When Eric finally loosened his grip on her (or was it the other way around?) so that our hostess could go in ahead of us, he hissed in my ear, "It's almost time you thought about losing a bit of weight, dear. Rebecca feels like a feather when you hug her."

"And what do I feel like," I hissed, "a bag of bricks?" Oh this was going to be an even longer night than I had expected. "I personally don't find anorexia especially appealing, unlike you."

Not thin, but just right, I had come to love my hour-glass body. It had taken many years and lots of odd diets to get to this point. I especially remembered with some disgust the boiled egg and

164

grapefruit diet that was all the rage at one point. I grimaced just thinking about it, but I had lost five pounds in two days. After four days, I had to stop it, since the weight was falling off and I had seriously bad breath, a headache and no energy. After that there had been a succession of Oprah-approved diets: the all-vegetable diet, the shellfish diet, the high-protein diet, the high-fibre diet, and the list went on. The latest craze was the gluten-free diet. Fortunately, by this time, I knew quite a bit about nutrition and was not going to succumb to madness this time around. I knew that it was only a matter of time before gluten-free diets were found to be lacking one kind of micro-nutrient or other and the Yuppies who had embraced it like manna from heaven would be onto the next newest thing. In the meantime I braced myself for the inevitable conversations around the buffet table about the relative dairy and gluten content of the various delicious morsels on offer.

Eric and I made our way into the living room to wishes of happy anniversary; then Eric, always mindful of his husbandly responsibilities, headed off to the bar to get me a drink. I was going to need one. I looked around, but couldn't see Isobel anywhere. I fervently hoped that she had not decided to abandon me for the new man leaving me essentially on my own this evening. Of course, she did tend to be late for these kinds of gatherings.

Eric returned to my side just long enough to deposit a cold glass of white wine in my hot little hand, and then he was off to network. I took a sip, savouring the coolness of the exquisite Meursault as it slid down my throat then made my way over to the table laden with elaborate crudités. I jabbed a mini carrot in the green dip and tried to take the pulse of the party.

As far as I'm concerned, every party has its own personality – even if two days later I can't tell one from another. I had long-ago made this my game for getting through interminable parties overloaded with inane small talk, most of which varied little from one party to the next. So, just was the complexion of this party? Would it be gossipy and catty? Happy, jolly and drunken? (This one would be rather rare in this group.) Would it be ostentatious and stuffy? I hoped not. This last one was my least favorite, yet was possibly the most common personality that we encountered in our social circle. At least if the party veered toward the gossipy it would have rhythm. If the party were stuffy it could be counted upon to put me to sleep long before Eric wanted to go home. The stuffier and more ostentatious the better as far as he was concerned. To me they were like the dying hours of the last emperor.

166

Despite the fact that I was one of the guests of honor, there were several guests whose identities were a mystery to me. Rebecca would, no doubt have her reasons for inviting them even though they had no idea who we were or why they should be celebrating some unknown couple's anniversary. Mystery guests, as titillating as they might be, however, made it more difficult to label the party this early in the evening. They were like the wild cards. So, I decided to continue my assessment by focusing on the attire of the guests I did know.

Personally, I was wearing my cocktail uniform: black. I contended that if one wore black, one could get away with wearing the same dress to at least three different parties and no one would notice. After three, you start to get "the look" of pity. On the other hand, if you wore the same red dress (or oxblood to be of the moment like Rebecca always was), everyone would remember and remark upon the fact that you seem to like red – that is code for the observation that you didn't seem to have much variety in the sartorial side of life. Rebecca, I had observed, never wore the same outfit twice to a party.

As I turned away from admiring Rebecca's new dress, Renée LaChance spotted me. I felt a bit like a voyeur who was about to be caught, but evidently she had no idea that she'd been spotted earlier in the liquor store parking lot. Naturally, I did not mention it.

"Hello, Alex! Happy anniversary," she said as she gave me a peck on each cheek, her Prada "*Candy L'eau*" perfume practically gagging me with its sickly sweetness.

As I inhaled, it was clear that it had been liberally sprinkled to mask the unmistakable scent of *eau de gin* which lingered. The mixture was just slightly nauseating. I stood back and surveyed the secret lush. She was wearing an exquisite turquoise, silk cocktail dress which already had a most unbecoming splotch of something in the center of the right breast. It did seem a tad early for such a mess.

"It's always lovely to see you, Renée," I said, as I put my wine glass between the two of us to reduce my proximity to the stink. I took a sip. "How are the children?"

"Perfect, as usual," she said brightly. "You really should consider having one or two, you know. You're not getting any younger as they say."

Before I could open my mouth to respond, she started to prattle.

"It's so fulfilling to watch them grow, you know. Oh, you wouldn't know, would you?" She suddenly hiccupped. Slapping a bejewelled hand over her mouth, she continued. "We just love taking part in all those things that make up their tiny
168

lives. You have no idea how full their schedules can be. I mean, there are ballet, and hockey, and extra tutoring. Well, the tutoring isn't because they are not doing well in school, because they are doing well in school. It's just, well, you know how hard it can be to get into a good university and a good medical school these days. Or maybe even a Harvard M.B.A. would be okay."

My eyes started to glaze over as I thought about all the retorts I could come up with. Her children were still in grade school for starters, and how did she know that her daughter didn't want to be an aesthetician, but that's not a question you can ask a Yuppie mother, is it? And I had seen her daughter. A ballerina she was not.

My lack of responsiveness didn't deter her. "And you know, going back to work has been the ultimate fulfillment. Now I really do have it all, as they say!" She paused just long enough to take a large sip of her drink, but not long enough for me to get in a word. "But of course you do need to stay at home with your children for at least the first five years, don't you think? Those nasty stories you hear about urine-smelling daycare centers and drunken nannies are all true, you know. I suppose if you're very careful about your nanny and have a nanny-cam, it might be okay, but those daycare centers." She sipped again as she contemplated, so I

169

opened my mouth. Too late. "You never can be quite sure what kind of other children they'll be exposed to," she continued. "I mean, they do need to be exposed to diversity I suppose – we do have play dates with children of several races. That's so important. But as a social worker I see so many products of these unsavory environments."

I tried to interject yet again, to no avail.

She continued unabated. "And it is best for the mother to be at home anyway, don't you think? I mean, if you want to work all the time, you really shouldn't have children, should you? But mothers should, of course, be paid to stay home, don't you think? I'm considering mounting a campaign. Oh," she said as if she had just thought of something wonderful, "You work for a public relations firm, don't you, Alex? I'm sure it would be just the kind of community activity that's so good for your company's image. I'd love to chat more about it. I'm sure your people would just love to provide a bit of *pro bono*? Anyway, this is hardly the place or time," she said hiccupping again.

I finally had an opening. "What about those women who truly enjoy their work? Isn't it their right to have a career? Why should everyone take five years off?" Why was I even engaging??

"Alex, you're starting to sound like one of those hard-core feminists. They've had their day, in case you haven't heard. It's very unbecoming. Most of those feminists are lesbians, you know."

"What…?" I started to interject.

"I am a social worker, after all. I see these things. Lesbians don't have this problem now, do they? Anyway, I'd be a bit more careful about these kinds of attitudes if I were you."

What kinds of attitudes?! I felt my jaw clenching and was about to blurt something that I would probably have regretted when my non-Yuppie self really kicked in and said: *You'll never change her.* This, I knew. Whenever Renée mounted her mile-high soapbox, look out below. She was always right, if you know what I mean. And it has to be said that Renée's two children were shining examples of Yuppie children. Now eight and six years old respectively, Joshua and Meggan had it all – at least all that grade-school-aged children can either own or do, that is.

Renée's obsession with having the perfect children had begun some years ago during her first pregnancy, and I had seen her behavior repeated time after time in other acquaintances since. She was nothing if not an early adopter.

The very moment her pregnancy became public knowledge, she started a whisper campaign against drinking during pregnancy. As far as I could figure out from actually reading the medical research which was more than Renée ever did, light drinking has no effect on developing fetuses, but that didn't stop the media and every pregnant Yuppie from feeling it was now their sacred duty to ensure that no woman who even so much as appeared to be pregnant ever held a drink in her hand. And as for smoking, well, it was best if those 'types' never crossed her path. But then there was the dietary evolution into the world of the peanut and gluten-free pregnancy (all of which has since been found to be bunk, but Renée will not be moved from her opinions).

She had read poetry to each of her children in utero, played Mozart and recited multiplication tables *ad nauseum*. Once ushered into the world, the little tykes had been hauled off to "baby bubbles" classes at the pool (at their private club), followed by baby-and-me yoga classes.

By the time little Joshua was three, he had been subjected to two hours of daily flash-card activities plus mornings at a Montessori school. Renée had then added music appreciation, and in an attempt to have a well-rounded child, she had added power skating, downhill skiing and I swear I saw him lugging a full-sized tennis racket one day. I knew all of this because Renée often complained about her exhaustion at the level of strict scheduling to which she was obliged to adhere. Once when I had suggested she might consider dropping something –

in fact I suggested once that she drop Meggan's ballet classes (the child looked to be on the verge of being a childhood obesity statistic), only to be told that little Meggan's ballet teacher had opined that she seemed to be quite talented and if she could just learn to touch her toes, all would be right in the world of ballet. After that I just smiled and nodded, making my get-away at the first possible opportunity.

As I was about to engage in the conversation, Robert joined our little tete-a-tete, and believe it or not, I was happy to see him for a change.

"Alex, my dear, you are ravishing this evening – as usual." He then did the double-kiss. He turned to Renée. "Perhaps you'd like a glass of Perrier, my dear?"

Renée poked her tongue out at him and stomped off toward the bar. I saw the bartender pouring her another large gin and tonic.

Robert put his arm on the small of my back. I moved it back down to his side.

"Your husband, he is a bit flirtatious this evening, no?"

The look on my face must have told Robert that I had not a single clue to what he was talking about. He continued. "I have just now seen him nuzzling the neck of a lovely lady in the dining room. Is that not unlike him?"

"I would believe almost anything of him this evening, Robert. He had a few drinks before we left the house. In fact, I had to drive." Robert had, however, piqued my curiosity about just how flirtatious my husband might be behaving out of my sight. I decided I should probably find out and keep a bit of an eye on him given his state of non-sobriety. He was up to something; I could feel it, and it was just a matter of time before I found out what it was.

Robert and I chatted amiably for a few more minutes while Renée, over in the corner accompanied only by her drink, got quietly drunker. I excused myself to go to the powder room. When I returned to the crowded living room, I spotted my wayward husband at the bar.

"Alex, my darling," he said as I took up position beside him. "Would you care for another drinky?" He hiccupped, and yet still looked meticulously groomed.

"Yes, perhaps a small one," I said. "That *Meursault* is very good." I took the glass from the bartender and sipped thoughtfully. Eric didn't seem to be particularly flirtatious to me. As a matter of fact, he seemed more subdued than he had before we left the house. "Are you having a good time?"

"Yes, as a matter of fact I am," he said. "I'm doing a small survey to determine the reading habits of our friends."

174

I turned abruptly away from my contemplation of the magnificent flower arrangement on the end of the bar, but Eric was busily engaged in receiving another drink from the bartender. I was now contemplating how many of my friends he might have asked about their experience of reading "50 Shades..." I shivered at the thought. What must they be thinking? I took a deep breath.

"And what are you discovering?"

"Well," he said sipping his drink as he leaned back against the bar, "a surprising number of our friends never read fiction."

"And why is this important to you?"

"I have always been interested in our friends' hobbies. You know that, Alex."

He was definitely up to something. Did he have any suspicions about my alter ego? No, that was impossible. It must just be a coincidence, but I had never believed in coincidence. Just then I noticed our hostess making her way directly toward us, the throng parting in her wake.

"There you are, you two love-birds "she said as she discovered the two guests of honor. "There are several people here I'd love for you to meet. After all, it is your party and you should know everyone!"

Rebecca took me by the hand and led me, with Eric following, through the living room, across the hall and into the den where a fire crackled in the fireplace. I could hardly believe it. The evening was still a scorcher, and here was Rebecca with a fire on and the air conditioning turned up.

As we were introduced to a selection of over-dressed, overly-made-up and overly gregarious guests, I wished that my notebook was handy. Olivia would just love this group. *(Oops, Olivia you are not supposed to infiltrate my life. We've talked before about this!).* In any case, I'd have to hold that thought.

TWELVE

As I listened to the conversations around me and noted that they seemed to be a repeat of every conversation I'd ever heard at a cocktail party before, I furtively glanced at my watch. We'd been here for an hour already and there was still no sign of Isobel. I needed her to rescue me from death by tedium. What could possibly have been keeping her? As much as I really did not want to run into Paul tonight – or any other night in this town for that matter – I had to admit to myself that I really did always look forward to seeing him. I could not get thoughts of him with my best friend out of my mind. Was I fearful that he might spill the beans about my secret before I was ready to do it myself? Or was I jealous? One thing was clear, I was going to have to come clean with Isobel and I was going to have to do it soon.

I sidled over to a little knot of people where Eric was holding court. Since he was acting so peculiarly this evening, he bore some oversight.

"Oh, here's my beautiful wife now," he said, gesturing for me to join him at the center of the group. "Your ears must be burning; we were just talking about you."

"Oh?" I said suspiciously.

"Yes. I was just relating to everyone some of the funny stories you've told me over the years about your clients."

I didn't quite know what to say. "Eric," I said smiling through gritted teeth, "you know that those stories are confidential." I looked around at the little group for reassurance that they agreed.

"Well, whatever. I was just telling them that you're a woman of wide-ranging interests. I learn more about my bride of ten years each day I'm married to her. There's nothing like a little mystery to keep the spark in a relationship, I always say!"

He had never been known to say such a thing. He was making me very nervous. He leaned over to try to kiss me. I ducked. At that moment, I was saved from further scrutiny from the assembled group by a commotion at the front door.

I heard Rebecca's voice, which seemed to be slightly shriller than it had been an hour ago – was she just a bit stressed, perhaps? Then I heard another one that was only vaguely familiar.

"Just flew into town, dear," the voice was saying. "Wish I had known you were having a swanky party; I would have worn one of my New York dresses." She laughed. "It was naughty of you to have overlooked our invitation, Beck."

There was only one person in the entire world that Rebecca could tolerate calling her anything other than Rebecca. It was Aunt Myra, otherwise
178

known as Mrs. Kenneth Silverman-Smith. AKA Rebecca's mother.

"I do wish Ken could have come with me tonight."

Ken was Myra's new husband, Rebecca's new step-father. I knew only too well what she thought of that union. Married three months ago, Myra and Ken, it seemed, had been on something of an extended honeymoon: Rebecca hadn't seen her since the wedding. In fact, I knew she hadn't seen her since some time before the wedding. They married in Vegas. I was trying to picture Aunt Myra at an Elvis-themed wedding chapel. It was making me a bit giggly.

Hoping that her mother would marry a nice, boring, rich, Jewish widower, Rebecca had done her level best to ensure that her mother met a series of eligible possibilities – the widowed fathers of every Jewish woman and man within a hundred-mile radius. In fact, she had asked my opinion once about what I might consider to be a suitable period of time to wait after a funeral to approach the widower with the prospect of a date. I had blanched at the very idea.

But Rebecca's efforts had been in vain. Myra, the independent sort that she was, had gone to Hawaii on vacation last winter and had met Ken Smith, a retired naval officer. Apparently he had been attending some sort of navy reunion in Maui where she had spotted him in his white uniform. That did it for her. According to Rebecca, ever since her father had died, her mother had never been able to resist a uniform. It didn't seem to matter what kind of uniform. She liked army officers, sailors, airline pilots, mall security guys and the occasional postal service worker it seemed. Then there was Ken, a nice, Catholic widower in a uniform. At least we had been told it was a naval uniform. Who really knew?

After a courtship of about two months, he had asked her to marry him and the rest, as they say, is history. I was only disappointed that I had not yet had the chance to meet Ken. I especially loved Aunt Myra, as I had been invited to call her, since meeting her at that Bat Mitzvah in Isobel's synagogue. Her vivacious personality and independent thinking endeared her to me. She was undeniably a woman to be reckoned with in my view. The party was definitely looking up, although from the look on Rebecca's face, she clearly didn't share my enthusiasm. Now if only Isobel would arrive, it could really get started!

Myra made her grand entrance into the living room by bursting through the archway to immediately take command of her space as she always did.

"Get me a drink, dear," she was saying to Rebecca as she pulled off her white kid gloves that she always wore. It was like her sartorial signature. For someone who didn't know there was a party here tonight, she was certainly dressed for the occasion.

Aunt Myra turned toward me. "Alexis, my dear, Rebecca tells me that all of this is in homage to your tenth wedding anniversary. You certainly merit congratulations on having stayed married to that dreary man for that length of time."

Rebecca turned on her heel and headed as quickly as she could toward the bar as I looked around to see who else might be listening. I especially wanted to see if Eric had heard her pronouncement. Eric despised Myra and as you can probably infer, the feeling was mutual. Eric had told me on more than one occasion how loud and obnoxious he thought Myra was and how someone of her age and girth should dress more age-appropriately. Myra for her part had told me in no uncertain terms that she found Eric to be cloying and superficial. I suppose it was difficult to argue with that.

I could see Eric approaching Myra from behind. His mouth was clenched into that phony smile that he had perfected for such occasions.

"Yes, and it's so lovely to see you again, too, Aunt Myra."

She flinched slightly: I knew that she loathed it when Eric called her that. She turned abruptly toward Eric. "Well, it isn't lovely to see you, Eric, and I don't for one moment believe that you think it's lovely to see me. A little honesty would suit you now and again, you know. I was actually hoping that you might have a dental emergency or have driven a drill into your clumsy hand this evening." She looked around. "Rebecca," she called as she moved off toward the bar, patting my arm in a kind of pitying way. "Where's that drink? I need it more than ever now."

Eric also moved away and I found myself standing alone beside David. It was my first opportunity that evening to chat with him. He was looking at Myra's retreating back as he sipped what looked to be a scotch on the rocks out of what appeared to be a kitchen glass rather than the hand-etched crystal that Rebecca had put out.

"You know, Alex, I sometimes wish that Rebecca was more like her mother," he said.

"I don't think I'd let her hear you say that, David. She seems to be a bit stressed by Myra's appearance here this evening."

David didn't seem to hear me. "You know, there are lots of people I wish Rebecca were more

182

like. You, for example, Alex. I wish Rebecca were more like you."

Surprised by his confession, I took my wine glass down from my lips and looked at him. I had long recognized that Rebecca had her limitations so to speak, but I had always thought that David saw them more as strengths in the kind of marriage that he seemed to need.

I must have looked very surprised.

"What I mean, Alex, is that Rebecca is so caught up in my life. For the last couple of years I've noticed that she seems to live her life vicariously through me. Don't get me wrong: she is the perfect "doctor's wife," but I sometimes wonder how that could be enough for her – or anyone else for that matter. Doesn't she ever wish for a life of her own? I mean, do you have any idea what it's like to have someone else's experience of life so dependent on yours? Sometimes it's terrifying." He gulped his drink. "Have you and she ever talked about that? I mean, you being a full-time career woman and all?"

"David, have you ever confided these concerns to Rebecca?"

David sat down on the arm of a wing-backed chair by the bay window where we were standing. Most of the guests seemed to have drifted off into the dining room by this point and we were almost

183

alone, with the exception of a couple of neighbors who were deep in conversation on the other side of this rather large room.

"She would never understand," he said. "She has a preconceived notion of what her – or our – life should be like. She doesn't like change, with the possible exception of her penchant for changing the décor of the house annoyingly often."

I wondered what was at the root of David's sudden onslaught of melancholia about his life and marriage. I had always thought that he rather liked his comfortable lifestyle and the predictability of having Rebecca always there for him – the perfect wife, mother and hostess. But I guess we don't really know what goes on inside other people's relationships – it's difficult enough to know what's going on inside our own. David had, in fact, never before confided in me. I wondered what was in the air on this hot, sticky night that was triggering this unburdening.

"There's not enough real excitement in life, you know, Alex. I mean, I love my work and my family, but I sometimes – no, strike that – I often wonder if this is all there is."

"It's a lot more than some people get in life, you know, David." It's funny, I had often thought that he and Rebecca had a somewhat shallow life, and here I was defending his own life choices to him. But then, it was becoming clear to me that
184

there was more to this than met the eye. None of my business, though.

"You know what our problem is, Alex?" he asked as he got up from the arm of the chair. "Our lives are too easy." He drained his glass. "And we all do too much navel-gazing." He walked toward the kitchen and disappeared into the inner sanctum with the caterer.

I stood there trying to make some sense out of what had just transpired then looked up to see a friendly face. Isobel had arrived. Finally. I smiled and relaxed just a bit as I hugged her. The sense of relaxation lasted but a moment as, over her shoulder I found myself eyeball to eyeball with Paul, my editor. So, he was really here. I swallowed hard and let go of my best friend.

Isobel looked especially lovely this evening. Not only were her clothes beautifully put together in a rather unorthodox way (I would not choose a pencil skirt with ankle boots but she would and did), but she had a bit of an uncharacteristic glow about her. For a very scary moment, I wondered if she might not be in love.

I tried frantically to analyze the thoughts and feelings that were whirling around in my head as if my brain were home to a blender. I had to put my finger on my feelings if I planned to be cool and collected at this turn of events. Paul and I had known one another for over five years. J. L. Kidston had actually started her publishing career with another editor in another publishing house, but had a bit of a disagreement about the level of eroticism that was necessary to pour onto the pages. J.L. (me) had the notion that there was a line between erotica and pornography – that editor saw no need to separate the two. So I separated myself from the editor. The subtleties of the narrative were a trademark of the J.L. Kidston brand. However, since the publication of "50 Shades..." it seemed that readers could handle upping the ante for eroticism. Anyway, Paul and I had found one another and ours had been a meeting of the minds ever since.

I had always found Paul extremely attractive – and I don't mean only in the looks department. Resembling a young Paul Newman, his looks were certainly passable (!), but it was his intellect, sense of humor and compassion that had hooked me from the start. The fact that we shared a lot of common interests didn't hurt either. For example, he didn't really care about fitting into a social mold, fundamentally dancing to the beat of his own drum. I envied him his life. He was content to make himself happy. Although that might sound a bit self-centered, it was actually less self-centered than the activities of members of my own social circle.

186

Paul had been recently divorced when I met him. He had wanted to have children, but his wife, a magazine editor on the fast-track, had adamantly refused. After we had gotten to know one another on editorial ground, we had become friends, sharing many a happy lunch of Thai food at one of his favorite haunts near his office. He told me about the women he dated, and I, the old married woman, tried to help him to understand what women want. I had never experienced even a moment of jealousy. Until now, that is. Why did it burn me so much to see him with my best friend? Maybe it wasn't jealousy at all, but my need to keep that part of my life separate and secret from this every day one. I should have been delighted that my two best friends seemed to have found one another. Oh well, my more imminent concern was that Paul not give me away. We were supposed to be strangers and he was bound to secrecy by the terms of my contract.

"Alex, I'd like you to meet Paul Cameron. You remember me telling you about him?"

Paul extended his hand while I tried not to look directly into his green eyes. "I'm delighted to meet you, Alex. Isobel has told me a lot about you. By the way, congratulations on ten happily married years. May you have ten more."

I swear I saw him wink at me. At least he wasn't going to do anything to give me away. I don't know what made me think he would. He was the consummate professional. Anyway, with the introductions over, as much as I longed to stay and chat with the two friendliest people in the place, I didn't trust myself so made my excuses and slid off to the powder room hoping to avoid Paul for the rest of the evening if at all possible. It would be difficult, though, since Isobel would rightly expect me to spend some time with her.

I sat on the toilet seat in Rebecca's chichi powder room with its black, flocked wallpaper and its mirrored vanity with my head in my hands. What was happening? After all this time something seemed to be changing – my world seemed to be shifting, or perhaps more to the point, my two worlds were on a collision course. I had to figure it out before I took a serious misstep.

My husband was acting very peculiar; my editor was becoming the bridge between the fantasy world I had created for myself and the real world I had to live in every day. My so-called friends seemed to have more problems than I could ever have imagined. What was going to happen?

Finally, someone knocked on the bathroom door, so I thought that I should check my lipstick and return to the madness.

When I walked into the dining room, I could see Rebecca's rear end sticking out from under the table as she furiously cleaned crumbs from the rug
188

with her hand-vac. Strange behavior, I thought. She was the kind of hostess who usually left these kinds of things to the hired help during parties. The next thing I knew, she was wiping unseen spots from the silverware with the hem of her dress.

"Oh, and by the way, Rebecca, while you're at it you might refill the pistachio trays in the living room and get rid of those disgusting sprout thingies that you're trying to pass off as munchies. But for the love of god, change those towels in the powder room. They are the most disgusting shade of puce I've ever seen. I cannot even dry my hands on them for fear the color might rub off."

I should have known: Aunt Myra was on the loose and seemed to have imbibed several glasses of champagne too many. And so Rebecca had regressed into the dutiful daughter that she claimed she was not, fulfilling her mother's every oddball demand.

"Rebecca, is there anything I can do to help?" I said as she swished past me on her way to refill the pistachio dishes.

"Of course not, darling," she said pushing a stray hair out of her eye. "You just have a good time."

"So where are you and Eric going for your vacation this year?"

I turned abruptly toward the voice in my ear. "Oh, hello Eleanor. I didn't see you there."

Eleanor St. John was slightly older than our usual crowd. This meant that she had a lot more Yuppie experience than the rest of us. She had a bigger house, more expensive car and more vacations under her belt about which she could talk for hours on end. And she did. She was tall and expensively dressed in a pair of what appeared to be maroon, silk lounging pajamas. But of course, pajama dressing was all the rage, wasn't it?

"You young career people!" she was saying both to me and to the admiring group surrounding her (admiring her; not me). "You really should learn to have a bit more fun. Always working!"

Eleanor liked the fact that she was older, although it does have to be said that she was only at most a decade older than most of us – hardly the silver-haired wise woman she pretended to be. She was probably right, though. We should have more fun in our lives; and if Eric and I actually liked each other at this very moment, we probably could have considered spending our tenth anniversary anywhere but here.

"Howard and I are going to Thailand, you know."

I didn't know, and I hadn't asked.

"We're spending four days in Hong Kong on the way. Four days is a minimum, you know."

190

I started to look around for an escape.

"It only takes two days for them to do me three custom dresses and two custom silk blouses, but there is so much other shopping to do, you know."

Again I didn't know, but the rest of her entourage smiled and nodded knowingly. The one of them asked her a question about some tailor or other in Hong Kong and I had my chance. I made a break away and found myself outside by the pool. No one was here since it was still warmer outside than inside in the air conditioning, although I could see a stage set up with musical instruments. Rebecca no doubt had a band that would appear when the air cooled a bit.

I took refuge behind a very large planter and sat down on a lounge chair. I closed my eyes.

"Having a good time?"

I was startled by a voice very close to my ear. My eyes opened and I saw Paul leaning over me, laughter dancing in his eyes. He stood up and shoved his left hand into his pocket and sipped the beer he was holding in his right. He grinned.

"Paul, you startled me! It is truly wonderful to see you, but we're not supposed to know one another," I said looking around stealthily.

He sat down on the lounger beside me placing his beer glass on the table between the two loungers. "We were properly introduced earlier, remember. I see no reason why I shouldn't be seen having a conversation with the guest of honor. Well, at least one of them. I already had the dubious pleasure of a blessedly brief conversation with the other one. Your husband is quite a character, isn't he? After all these years, and all the things you've told me about him, I felt like I knew him. It seems you have him pegged quite correctly. But you never told me that he drinks. It seems a bit out of the character sketch you painted."

"It's more than a little out of character," I said sitting up straight. "He's up to something this evening; I just can't seem to figure out what it is. I'm beginning to think he's having an affair. I'm not sure I'm wrong."

"An affair?" Paul started to laugh. "I don't mean to be unkind, J.L…"

"Sshhh! Don't call me that!"

"…Alex, then. What kind of a woman would sleep with him?"

"Someone like me, maybe? He's not always that repulsive."

"Sorry. I didn't mean it that way. I was out of line. Am I forgiven?" He leaned over and kissed me fully on the mouth. To say that this surprised me would be something of an understatement. Paul and I didn't have that kind of relationship – or at least I didn't think we did. It was par for the course, as they say, though. This was turning out to be the

192

weirdest evening I had ever spent. When would it just be over?

"By the way, Paul, whatever are you doing in town? "

"I'm looking for lakefront property, and some of the best is only an hour out of town."

I was slightly alarmed. Paul living that close to me? I could almost feel my comfortable secret fantasy live unravelling. Something would have to be done.

Paul glanced at his watch – he was one of those old-fashioned kind of guys who didn't click on a cell phone for the time. I loved him for that.

"I guess I had better get back inside. Isobel will be wondering what happened to me. Talk to you later?" he said as he got up and ran his hand through his thick hair.

Before I could say anything he had evaporated into the house and I was alone with my thoughts again.

The party had not lived up to Olivia's expectations. The people were dull, the conversations tedious. Even the champagne bubbles seemed lazy. She walked out onto the terrace with its commanding view of the Hudson River, placed her half-empty champagne flute on a table and took in the glittering lights. Were they a bit duller? Or

was that her imagination. Everything lacked
sparkle. The infinity edge swimming pool that
seemed to fall off into oblivion was illuminated by
lights of ever-changing hues. She sat down in one
of the loungers contemplating the changing lights.
A swim, perhaps, she thought. The lack of a
bathing suit was never an impediment to Olivia.
She arose, kicked off her Monolos and languidly
peeled off her cocktail dress. Her lack of lingerie
made the activity even simpler. She slid silently
beneath the surface so as not to attract attention.
When she surfaced, she could see two feet clad in
high-gloss brogues very close to the edge of the
pool. She slowly swam under water to the far side
where the water seemed to be one with the night sky
and surfaced again. She glanced back toward
where the shoes had been. They were gone.
Suddenly he was beside her, coming up from
beneath the water, his naked body bathed in the
shifting colors. Red, then blue, then green. She
could feel his hand on her back, but she didn't turn
to see his face. She would not see the face this time
and knew that her explorations were not over.

THIRTEEN

I wandered back into the house. Rebecca's imitation of a southern plantation slave was becoming irritating. Every time anyone placed a glass down on anywhere, she was there. Either she picked it up and ran to the kitchen if it was empty, or she slid a coaster under it. I had never seen anything like it. Myra, on the other hand, after telling Rebecca about the evils of air conditioning, had evidently turned it off and ensconced herself beside an open window as the temperature began to rise. It was only a matter of time before everyone retreated to the pool deck.

Minutes later it seemed, the orchestra had taken up their places by the pool and the music began. Despite my various strategies for the evening, there was now no way I would be able to avoid Eric any longer. Although he really did despise dancing, when in a drunken stupor, much like Toronto's mayor Rob Ford, all bets were off. And tonight he was in as close to a drunken stupor as I had ever seen him. I knew that in his inebriated state he could be counted on to do a few turns around the dance floor. Since we were the guests of honor, I knew that Rebecca would expect us to have the first dance, like at a wedding. Dear god!

Neither one of us was a particularly good dancer, although I did love to be led around a dance floor by someone who really knew what he was doing. Eric was not that person. To add to the misery, Eric's usual self-consciousness about letting others see him do things at which he did not excel seemed to have evaporated somewhere between the multiple drinks he had consumed at home and the continuing refills he was imbibing since our arrival. So we danced.

He must have been watching more television than I had thought: his dance moves seemed to have improved. Or did this explain the ticket stubs I had found in his jacket pocket? Had he really gone to a downtown dance club without me? Why had he been there? Perhaps more to the point in my view just at that minute, who had been his companion? I was now more determined than ever to find out.

"So, where did you learn those new dance moves, Eric?" I whispered into his ear as we moved together.

"Oh, do you like them?" he said rather more loudly than I had hoped. "I've been watching music videos when you're out. Trying to keep up with the new music scene." He was starting to breathe heavily.

"And here was me thinking that you'd been to a dance club. Maybe the Hidden Monkey," I said.

"Good god, Alex! You know I wouldn't be caught dead in a place like that. It's not our kind of place." He moved out of earshot for a moment.

Since others had now joined us on the dance floor and were not paying the slightest bit of attention to us, I decided to go for broke. "Then how do you explain the ticket stubs I found in the pocket of the jacket you asked me to take to the cleaner for you? They didn't get there on their own."

He stopped dancing and started to laugh in a drunken sort of way. "Is that what's been bothering you all evening? You've been acting very peculiar and this would explain it. I suppose you think I'm having some kind of sordid little affair or something. Maybe with a teenager? Or maybe my hygienist!" He was really laughing now – that snorting kind.

I had not actually thought of his hygienist. Was he saying that to put me off the trail? Then I thought about Susan. She'd been with him since forever. She was one of those older women of indeterminate age who was broad as she was tall with the most stereotypical of spinster habits you could imagine – cats and everything. But what lurked beneath that façade I now began to wonder? But then there was his new receptionist, Clara. She was a pretty twenty-year old who hung on his every word. What man approaching middle age wouldn't be attracted to that – not to mention the blonde bob and the long legs? She was the sort whose intellect wouldn't get in the way in any case.

"Maybe not Susan," I said, "but Clara. I'm sure the Hidden Monkey is just her sort of place on a Saturday night."

"I am deeply wounded, Alex, wounded to the core of my being."

"Don't you think you're being a bit melodramatic?" I said looking around to be sure we were not attracting any attention. We weren't. "I mean, to your core?"

"Melodramatic? Me? I suppose you also think I'm over-reacting." (I did.) "For your information, my darling wife, I am not now nor ever have been unfaithful to you. I think it's very demeaning to be accused by one's wife on the occasions of one's tenth wedding anniversary of something the sort of which one has never contemplated."

I was starting to lose track with all of the third-person references. Were we still talking about Eric?

"Well, what exactly have you contemplated? This still doesn't explain how those ticket stubs got into your pocket."

"I picked them up off the lawn, if you must know." He was pouting now. Then he sighed and turned to walk away from me toward the house – and the bar beyond, no doubt.

198

I followed him. "I wish you wouldn't do that."

He turned back toward me, stopping briefly. "Do what?"

"Walk away from me when we're having a serious discussion. You don't always get to decide when the conversation is over."

"Alex, there is nothing serious about a discussion wherein there is not a shred of truth or trust. I am going to the bathroom and I don't relish having company."

So apparently he did get to decide when the conversation was over. I was seething. But the more I thought about it, the more I considered that his explanation probably was true. The truth was that he certainly was OCD enough to pick up even the tiniest bit of detritus that might have fallen onto his small patch of lawn. In fact, Eric being Eric, that was a more plausible explanation. I was almost disappointed in how boring this was. I still didn't quite trust him this evening, though; his overall behavior was making me more and more uncomfortable. I sighed and turned back to the pool deck.

Rebecca was heading toward me again, this time with an older, very distinguished-looking gentleman in tow. He was over six feet tall with a shock of silver hair that was just slightly tousled. He was wearing a crisp, cream-colored linen sport jacket (there's an oxymoron: crisp linen!) over an open-necked, deep sapphire blue polo with the collar just turned up ever so slightly. He reminded me of a grown-up 1970's preppy. He was smiling.

It was strange to be the guest of honor at a party where I knew only about two-thirds of the guests; he was one of the unknowns, but the way Rebecca was steering him in my direction, I knew that I was about to be introduced. I assume that all of this was Rebecca's doing: David usually just showed up and paid the bills.

Rebecca opened her mouth as she reached me at exactly the same moment that Robert and Renée materialized at my side and started to chat up a storm. I wasn't listening. I was watching Robert who smiled in recognition at the man Rebecca was about to introduce. Was I the only one who didn't know who he was?

Robert held out his hand to the stranger. "J.B., what a pleasant surprise," he was saying as they shook hands.

J.B.'s face suggested that he didn't seem nearly as happy to see Robert as Robert seemed to be to see J. B.

"I had no idea you and the Rubenstein's were friends! Or perhaps," Robert said and then turned toward me, "you are friends with the guests of honor? Where is your lovely wife this evening?" He looked around.

200

J.B. scowled at this last remark. Before he could respond, Rebecca interrupted to make the introduction.

"Alex, I'd like you to meet Jonathan MacDonald. Jonathan is an old friend of David's family." She turned toward Jonathan, aka J.B. "Jonathan, I believe you already know Alex."

Jonathan obviously recognized the puzzled look that no doubt fleetingly flitted across my face. Although it was clear I had no idea who he was, he gallantly came to my rescue.

Taking my hand to his lips he said, "Really only by reputation, my dear Rebecca." He actually kissed my hand, holding it for what might be considered a moment too long as Robert looked on with interest.

This revelation did not clear up his identity for me in the slightest. I hoped he'd say something more so that I could get a handle on his identity. Why did he know me by reputation? What reputation? I could feel the hairs on the back of my neck start to rise. Had he been talking to Paul? Was the jig, as they say, up? He knows my secret, I was thinking, and he's about to spill.

God love, Robert, as he chimed in. "J.B., you remember my wife Renée, do you not?"

"Can't say that I do, Robert, but I'm glad to meet you now, Renée." He quickly kissed her hand.

"I'm happy to see you again," Renée gushed. "I mean, we only met briefly a couple of years ago." She hiccupped rather alarmingly. "But Robert talks about you all the time."

I still didn't know who J.B. was, and I certainly had no idea about the connection between him and Robert. I was feeling dumber by the minute and didn't know how to extricate myself. I should simply ask how he knew me, but I feared the answer. Not knowing who knew what about whom and why was becoming very perplexing.

"I gather you two know each other," I said finally.

"But, of course, Alex, J.B. is the senior partner at my firm. He also happens to be on the board of one of your largest clients. You know this, yes?"

I looked at Jonathan – J.B. – for affirmation.

He laughed. "You probably don't know, Alex, but I'm the chairman of the board of Lunar Botanicals. I keep a low profile. But I do know quite a bit about you."

The fact that he was chairman of the board of the newest (not, as Robert might think largest) client at Lander Pearson made me feel slightly better, but his last remark put me on guard again.

"Oh, and what do you know about Alex?" Rebecca asked.

She asked the question I could not, but certainly wanted to.

202

"Well, it just so happens that Alex is my daughter's boss and mentor. It's because of Alex that she plans to go back to school this fall to study marketing. Her mother," he glanced at Robert for a split second, "and I are delighted. She took that secretarial course after high school, but we always knew that she was born for greater things."

Pam's father! Great waves of relief were washing over me. I was so relieved at this revelation it was all I could do to keep myself from throwing my arms around his neck and kissing him. As I started breathing, I realized that I had been holding my breath.

Before I could respond, a striking-looking older woman with fiery red hair slid in beside J.B. and put her hand on his arm. "There you are darling," she said. "What have I missed?"

"I was just talking about Pam and her decision to go back to school." J.B. then introduced me to Pam's mother who bore a striking resemblance to her daughter, if I squinted and pretended that this attractive older woman was wearing large, dark-rimmed glasses.

"You know, when Pam decided to forego college to take a few years to find herself, we were very worried," said Camilla, Pam's mother. "Then after she started working with you, we hoped that she might find a mentor in you. We were delighted when she told us just recently that she planned to pursue journalism as a direct result of your influence."

I was flattered that Pam had thought enough of me to have talked about our work to her parents.

"You know, Alex," said J.B., "Pam is our pride and joy – a late baby as it were. She turned twenty-two last Sunday."

Just then, Robert whose attention had wandered off some time earlier started choking on an olive. Gin started to spurt out through his nose.

J.B. looked at him. "Thought I was too old to have daughter that young, did you, LaChance? " Then he turned to me. "She was the best thing that ever happened to our lives." He said as Camilla nodded. "Were thought we were too old to be parents ourselves, but there you are! If anyone were to hurt that young woman, they'd be at the mercy of my wrath! I'd kill to protect her!" He laughed.

Robert cleared his throat of the inhaled olive before he managed to speak. "So, J.B., what's it really like to have a young adult child these days? Do they still tell their parents everything? I mean, does she tell you who she dates?"

Where in the world was this going, I wondered. But perhaps more to the point, where was it coming from?

"She tells us everything," Camilla said as she reached for an hors d'oeuvre from a silver tray carried by a passing waiter.

I watched as she carefully popped it into her mouth without ever smudging her perfect lipstick. Then I looked at Robert who was looking a bit green. Perhaps he had inhaled too much gin. "Do you know Pam, Robert?"

"How would I know her," he said, rather too loudly. He abruptly turned toward his wife. "Shall we dance?"

"No, thanks," Renée said, yawning. "I think I'll just pop over to the bar and see what that bar tender is mixing now. Why don't you dance with Alex?"

Before I could say anything, Robert was strong-arming me toward the band. "What is the matter with you?" I said. "First you gush all over Jonathan, then you choke, then you can't wait to get away."

"Alex," he stage whispered to me, "I think I may be in big trouble. I may confide in you, yes?"

We had started to dance in that awkward way that non-dancers have when they are with a new partner. "I wish you would." It occurred to me that anything that Robert might confide might actually clear up a few oddities of the evening.

"I do know Pam."

At that point, this revelation didn't actually come as a surprise to me. I always prided myself in my author's ability to see beyond the surface of conversations – to read body language.   Robert's body language was speaking volumes.

"How well do you know her?"

Robert didn't answer immediately, so I waited until I could wait no longer. "You're having an affair with that young woman, aren't you?"

"I just said I knew her. We are just…friends."

"So, if you're just friends, what's the problem? Surely her father won't 'kill' you for that?"

Of course I had begun to put the pieces of the puzzle together in my head. Pam confided her secret to me. Robert was confiding a secret – sort of.

"Alex, you cannot tell anyone of this. You especially must not confide in Renée."

The music stopped. I pulled Robert over to a quiet corner behind a potted palm.   "Robert LaChance, you know very well that I'm perhaps the only person in this house this evening who wouldn't feel the necessity to broadcast someone else's affairs." He flinched at the word. "But I am close to Pam – and she and I do talk about personal things occasionally."

"Has she told you about me?"

"Not about you specifically, but I have a very good idea of what this is all about. Perhaps I have a
206

better idea even than you do. Anyway, I'm going to give you some advice whether you want it or not." He slumped down onto a chaise. I continued. "You had better get your marriage straightened out, and fast."

"There is nothing wrong with my marriage."

"I'm not finished. Whether you want to believe it or not, there is something drastically wrong with a marriage where the husband finds it necessary to sleep with young women while the wife gets drunk." He started to protest, but I stopped him. "You may believe that all of your problems are private, but you know as well as I do that life even in paradise has some venomous snakes. There is no one who does not face the consequences of his actions at some point. It's not my place to tell Renée anything. It's yours, and I fear your troubles might just be starting." I turned and stalked back into the house. I was furious at him.

The house was nearly empty at this point. Even Aunt Myra had gone out, if not to dance, then perhaps to give Rebecca further instructions. I was getting more and more tired of this party by the moment, but knew that I would probably be stuck here until the bitter end.

I wandered into the den where a vaguely familiar man was sitting at the end of the sofa deeply engrossed in what appeared to be a medical journal. He didn't notice me so I stood there for a few moments trying to figure out where I had seen him before. As I racked my brain, I decided to get a drink before engaging him in conversation as I thought a guest of honor ought to do.

When I returned, I found him in conversation with Eric who was hovering over the open journal, drink in hand, rocking slightly from side to side. He looked up.

"Alex, come over here and meet Sandy." He hiccupped. "He's gay, you know."

I was appalled to say the least. "Sandy, I'm Alex and this drunken man is my husband who is an ass."

Sandy smiled and I remembered where I had seen him before.

"Don't worry, Alex, he's actually right. I am gay, although that's not usually the way I'm introduced. People usually introduce me as a philosophy professor."

"So, who are you here with?" Eric asked. "We don't actually have any gay friends."

"At least not that you know of," I said, sotto voce. Eric didn't hear me, but Sandy did.

"What's going on here?" David came into the den carrying two glasses of kir royale. Handing one to Sandy, he looked at Eric. "Are you harassing the guests, Eric?"

"No," said Sandy. "Eric was just telling me that he doesn't have any gay friends." He seemed to be smirking.

"Maybe he just doesn't know who's gay and who isn't," I said.

"Oh contraire, my dear," Eric said, "I would most certainly know. You know there's such a thing as gaydar?"

I squeezed David's hand. "Yes, but it's something in which you are completely lacking, Eric."

David looked at me and then at Sandy who was smiling. I whispered to David. "Your secret is safe with me – but I'd think about coming out."

David nodded gravely.

"But I didn't necessarily mean this evening."

David looked at Sandy and they both smiled. Dear god, what had been unleashed this evening?

"You're making quite an ass of yourself, Eric," I said pulling him toward the door. "Let's go back outside."

When I pulled him back out to the pool deck he shrugged me off muttering something about another drink. I sighed. What an evening!

FOURTEEN

Stewed. Pie-eyed. Sh*t-faced. Whatever word you choose – many are the ways I could describe the people around me at the party. My own head was spinning, but not from alcohol. I was thinking about the perfect little world that Eric had built for himself – that I had knowingly entered, if not without qualms – and that seemed to be acquiring cracks by the minute.

Eric had chosen to be a dentist based not on a deep-seated desire to improve the dental health of the world; rather he had chosen it to line his pockets. He had systematically examined various occupations where he had the best opportunity to make the most money. He had considered various medical specialities where the money might be better, but the hours were not. There would be no on-call for him as he built his practice and bank account. He had briefly considered law, but the market for lawyers had all but dried up. Business had a certain appeal, but he only way to make real money was to own a successful business of your own – he never said it, but it was clear that he lacked the necessary creativity. Dentistry, however, required only an initial expenditure of money to equip an office, hire a couple of staff members, and then make as much money as one desired working

210

the number of hours one chose to work. He had often said that dentistry was the ideal profession because people would call him "doctor" while he had time and money to pursue his various interests – expensive cars, skiing, vacations and buying organic food at Whole Foods. For years this had been close to the truth.

After Eric had made that decision, he had been at least half way toward becoming a real Yuppie – not a 1980's type Yuppie, though. The Yuppie of the twenty-first century was a new and improved version. At least that's what Eric always thought. Once when I called him a Yuppie to his face, he got agitated and told me he certainly was not.

Eric, of course, needed a wife to complete the acquisitions. More and more just lately, it had occurred to me that I was probably one of his less appropriate decisions for furthering his reputation.

In addition to me, though, Eric's world was filled with an assortment of others who, as far as I could figure out, shared his vision of the world. And in that world, things rarely rocked the boat. People did not go bankrupt or lose their houses, no one did anything illegal (at least not that anyone else ever knew about), no one had to bail the teenaged children out of jail, no one got caught smoking crack (if it happened, it happened in private), no one got fat (or at least not very fat), no one had a heart attack, and presumably no one died. Now I'd have to add to that list that no one ever cheated on his wife with a man. Was tonight some kind of a watershed?

I wandered back outside scanning the crowd as I went. Was I really the only one who wasn't drunk? I walked around the perimeter of the swimming pool and found Eric continuing his discussion with David and Sandy. David did not look happy. I couldn't hear what they were saying, but they did seem to be arguing. As the voices started to rise, others milling around began to pay attention.

Rebecca, the perfect hostess, was serving drinks on the other side of the pool. She looked over, alarm etched on her face. Robert, who seemed to be avoiding his wife, looked over from where he was standing by himself near the door. Renée spotted him and made a bee-line toward her husband, tripping over Isobel's foot along the way. Paul, who was standing with Isobel and two other guests, looked over at me.

"You are so full of shit," I could hear David saying. It sounded so unlike him.

I wondered if I should go over to referee, although to tell the truth, I really wanted to stay out of the whole thing. I walked slowly toward the group. Just as I was about to say something, David said rather more loudly than might have been necessary under the circumstances. "Yes, Eric, Sandy is gay…and so am I."

All conversation in the vicinity stopped. Heads turned. Jaws sagged.

Oh no, I thought. Rebecca! This is not how someone should find out that her husband is sleeping with a man. But when I looked over at her, she seemed to be eerily calm.

"You should be ashamed of yourself!" Renée whose advance toward her husband had been stopped in its tracks by David's pronouncement, shrieked. "It isn't bad enough that you're cheating on your wife – but with a man!"

"I think you've had enough to drink for one evening, Renée," David said.

"Enough to drink? Well, at least my husband is faithful!"

David lowered his voice. "Your husband may not be sleeping with a man," he said, "but perhaps you should ask him who he *is* sleeping with."

Renée began to turn so pale that I thought she might throw up.

Eric, who was now beside me, seemed surprisingly coherent for someone who had imbibed so much liquor this evening. "Everyone seems to have their sordid little secrets that eventually get out, don't they darling?"

He seemed to be taking all of this upheaval in his well-ordered life uncharacteristically well. He had to have a breaking point, as did we all, and I hoped to get him out of here and home before it hit.

Myra, who had been listening all the while, had started in on Rebecca again, and she ws not taking her mother's input well.

"No, Mother, I'm not devastated. It so happens that I've known about David and Sandy for some time." With that, she turned around and walked briskly into the house leaving Myra, and the rest of us, slack-jawed.

"Quite a spectacle, don't you think?" Isobel and Paul had materialized by my side. "This party just might go down in the annals of entertaining as the most amusing in the history of this bunch!" She was absolutely gleeful. "So, who do you suppose will be the next confessor?"

I shuddered to think.

"Think I'll get myself a refill," Paul said, leaving us alone.

"Perhaps we should jump in," Isobel said.

"Huh? Jump in"

"Into the pool. It might get everyone's mind off the seriously weird pronouncements going on here tonight. Anyway, I've always known that David was gay. I'm actually delighted that he's finally come out of the closet." Isobel walked over

214

to the pool, kicked off her sparkly sandals, sat down and dangled her feet into the water.

I followed her, kicked off my not-so-sparkly sandals and joined her on the side of the pool, enjoying for a moment the feeling of the cool water on my toes. "You knew?"

"Yes. Back in university he swore me to secrecy. I tried to talk him out of marrying Rebecca.

"She knew back then?"

"Of course. It's a bit like Cole Porter, don't you think? His wife went along with it to protect his reputation. But that sort of thing always does come back to bite you in the butt eventually. Some secrets are just too big to keep."

I shuddered in spite of the heat and humidity of the waning evening. I looked up to see Aunt Myra making her way toward us.

"Well, girls," she said taking up position on a lounge chair beside us, "quite a party."

"Yes, indeed it is, Myra. Quite lovely," Isobel said. "You don't seem nearly as upset by David's announcement as I thought you'd be."

"To tell you the truth Izzie, I've always suspected as much. Theirs has always appeared to me to be a sexless marriage. I've mentioned it to Rebecca several times over the years, but she puts me off, playing the prude. She says it's not the sort of thing one talks to one's mother about."

"Well, I suppose she has a point," I said.

"Anyway, I have always feared that this day would come, although I knew it must." Myra turned to me. "Alex, I'm so sorry that it had to ruin your anniversary celebration."

"To tell you the truth, Aunt Myra, the party is a bit of a ruin for me anyway."

"Going to dump him, are you?"

I was taken aback by Myra's forthrightness. "Dump Eric?"

"Who else? The more I get to know him, the more I think he's a dipstick. You deserve better." She looked up at the guests whose numbers I had expected to dwindle at this point. It seemed as if they all wanted to stay around to see what else might happen. "You know, girls, this is really a tight-assed, pompous group of Yuppies as far as I can see."

Isobel and I both started to laugh.

"It's really no laughing matter, you know," Myra said, sounding just slightly miffed. She stood up. "Well, I think I'll go for a dip."

With that announcement, she kicked off her own shoes and jumped into the pool fully clothed causing a mini tidal wave. That got the crowd's attention.

216

FIFTEEN

Before I knew it, Isobel had joined Myra in the pool. This was followed by a tsunami of other drunken revellers flinging themselves in one after the other. I just hoped that none of them drowned, as soused as they all appeared to be.

Not feeling the need for a dip myself, I got up and wandered unnoticed into the house. The huge, incongruously ultra-modern Grandfather clock in the Rubenstein front foyer chimed midnight; it occurred to me that the party had just about reached disaster proportions. With half the guests now frolicking in the pool with their clothes on, and the other half coming apart at the seams, I thought that the night would never be over. It would be one anniversary to remember. But it wasn't over yet.

While Isobel and Aunt Myra splashed about in the pool, Paul had evidently been amusing himself by wandering through the house and garden observing the players, and listening in on conversations. By the time he found me once again emerging from the powder room where I had been for the better part of a quarter of an hour to regroup, he had a pretty good idea of what this crowd was all about – and he told me.

As I mentioned earlier, Paul was the one person who couldn't have cared less what other people thought of him. That alone disqualified him as a Yuppie. He was conventional enough when necessary – one did have to get along in the world, he had said to me more than once – but the idea of living each day caring about the thoughts, beliefs and material acquisitions of others left him cold. He was Eric's polar opposite in so many ways. It seemed that at this point in my life I had more in common with him than with my own husband of ten years. But it had not always been this way with Eric.

I had met Eric some twelve years earlier when I was just getting my career off to a real start. As long as there are public relations students and graduates in the world, there will always be Yuppies, and I was a new PR girl, so succumbed to the aspirational lifestyle at first. It was in that frame of mind that I met Eric, a newly minted dentist whose practice I stumbled upon in the yellow pages when searching for a new dental hygienist. He asked me out, we dated for a year and a half, and when he asked me to marry him, it seemed like to the right thing to do to say yes. Unfortunately, after the glow of the honeymoon in Hawaii which was *de rigeur* at the time, I was left with a palpable hole in my life. I subsequently filled it with the ravings of my over-active imagination.

218

I had begun writing within a year of the wedding and was published just after our second wedding anniversary. As I looked back from the vantage point of ten years in the trenches (of marriage), I realized that I might not have stayed married to Eric if I had not had my "other life." It struck me like a bold of lightning that I was now seriously considering making a major change in my life.

These were my thoughts when I emerged from the powder room to find Paul passing down the hall. He was, of course, charming as usual, almost irresistible in his own way, but as a friend of course. As I closed the bathroom door behind me, he put his arm around my shoulders and told me it was about time he and I had a real talk this evening. After all, what were friends for? He knew that I had "things" on my mind, he was saying to me.

We walked wordlessly for a moment, looking for a private place to chat. We finally settled on a quiet spot outdoors, far away from the pool deck in Rebecca's professionally-tended rose garden. Lit by the moon overhead, the path to the cement bench was clear. Many of the rose bushes, as early in the season as it was, were in full bloom, displaying varying shades of pink, Rebecca's favorite color. We sat down side by side.

"How do you fit into this bizarre group, Alex?"

"You'd be surprised how often I ask myself that very question," I said. "I guess it's just something that happens." To tell the truth, I was actually feeling a bit embarrassed about the whole evening, especially about the appearance of having had so little control over the evolution of my own life.

"This is not how I picture you, Alex. I've actually thought for a long time that you probably shouldn't have to lead this double life you've chosen. Now I know I'm right. You should have your picture on every book cover, on every web site that mentions you, on J.L. Kidston's Twitter feed. The whole nine yards. Your fans should know you. They're loyal and they deserve it; frankly, so do you."

I knew that he was right; I think I had known it for some time. I just didn't know how to rock the boat without ruining Eric's life; at least that's the excuse I had used for some years now. At this moment, it just looked conceited, as if his happiness somehow rested on my shoulders. What nonsense!

"I know you're right, Paul, but I've gotten used to the life I've been leading. It's comfortable," I said a bit too defensively. Comfortable? Really? Who was I kidding?

"I hope you're listening to yourself," Paul said, laughing. "Because I'm listening. I've always been listening. You've told me enough about your life

220

for me to know now that it's been affecting you as a writer and as a person. The truth is that I really didn't know the half of it until Isobel synchronistically enabled me to see the merry-go-round in the flesh."

"So, what about Isobel?" I said, changing the subject.

"What about her? We were talking about you."

"Are you two developing some kind of relationship?"

"You say that as if it's a bad word."

I could tell that he was needling me.

"I suppose we develop a kind of 'relationship' with everyone who becomes a part of our lives, even if that part is small and short-lived."

He wasn't really answering my question and he knew it.

"I know it's none of my business, Paul, but are you and Isobel romantically involved?"

"Would you mind?"

I wasn't really sure if I minded or not. I only knew that I had to know. After all, I counted the two of them as my two best friends in the world. The more I thought about it, the more it did seem like a good idea if they had found one another.

"All right," he said finally, "Isobel and I met on a plane a couple of months ago as she's probably told you. She is the original free spirit in my view;

that appealed to me right from the start. I think I found it especially endearing since she's a lawyer. I don't think I've ever seen that in a lawyer before. Then I found out that she is a rabid J. L. Kidston fan. When she told me where she lived, I put the picture together and couldn't resist finding out if she knew you." He must have seen the startled look on my face. "Don't worry. She has no idea I know you, much less work with you. Anyway, when she began telling me about her friend Alex, I knew that I just had to get her to invite me somewhere you'd be. It actually happened sooner than I thought it would."

"So that story about you looking for lakefront property is just a ruse?"

"No, that's actually true. I really am looking for some place to build my dream house. I have a dream of telecommuting to my editorial job some day – after I have a family."

"I thought you'd given up the idea of having a family."

"I thought so, too." He suddenly looked very serious. "Never lose sight of your dreams, Alex. They may be all you have left some day."

I knew exactly what he meant.

"Enough of this seriousness," he said brightly. "Tell me about the new book. I can hardly wait to read it."

And so we moved on to our favorite topic of conversation – my writing projects. We fell naturally into our usual collegial camaraderie. Paul always came up with the most outrageous suggestions for increasing the eroticism in my books (much like my original editor had done, but in a much nicer way), and I always found a way around them. I had to be true to my own voice, and he knew it. He was probably the best editor in the world.

We were so deeply engrossed in our conversation that I hadn't noticed Isobel standing a couple of yards away, towel wrapped around her, leaning against the house. I smiled and waved her over, not initially realizing that she probably overheard at least a portion of our conversation. I now realized that my confession was imminent; I only hoped it wouldn't alienate her. After all, you don't really expect your best friend to keep such a juicy secret from you.

Apparently after Isobel and Myra had emerged from the pool and towelled off, she had noticed that both Paul and I were missing, so had gone in search of us. When she found us, she had observed two people deep in a conversation that didn't look as if they had just met, so she said. In fact, she said, we looked like two people who knew one another rather well. So, she had decided not to intrude. She had decided to eavesdrop. Had she heard much of our conversation? You bet she had. She had gotten more than an earful, but still had unanswered questions.

"Finding out that my best friend isn't who she has appeared to be might be the most difficult confession of the evening," she said, clearly distraught.

I stood up. "Isobel, I'm still the same person as I've always been. I'm exactly who you think I am. It's just that there's a little bit more to me than you knew about. I've been going to tell you for…well, forever. I never meant for it to be a secret from you. Just from everyone else. It's just that I got into the habit of dealing with my secret this way, and it got harder and harder to let anyone else in on it."

She looked at me suspiciously. "You've been lying to me for all these years. You even let me give you one of your own books!"

"I actually thought it was very sweet of you, and frankly it was that particular gesture that helped me to make up my mind that I could tell you – that you wouldn't be mortified by who I am. I was going to tell you – and soon. I just didn't expect it to come out by you overhearing it."

"Are you accusing me of eavesdropping? Well, I was." Then she smiled. "So, now J.L., 'fess up. I want the whole story. Don't spare a single detail."

So I told her. I started from the beginning and told her about my need to write, my first publishing experiences, my first encounter with Paul, how we had developed a friendship over the years, and about my upcoming book. By the time I had finished, the three of us were laughing and I was feeling a whole lot better about the evening. She was particularly astounded to discover that Paul was, in fact, my editor.

"Alex, you must have thought me quite a fool over the years to have suggested stories for J.L. Kidston." Isobel said finally.

"As a matter of fact, many of your suggestions were put to good use. You probably have never recognized many of your recommendations, but there were there, buried in my own plots and characters. You often made me think about a particular story line in a new way. So, thanks."

Isobel seemed thrilled with this. She seemed truly happy to be even a small part of something that was so dear to her heart, namely J. L. Kidston novels. I was delighted, and always had been, that my books brought her so much entertainment over the years. She sat down on the bench between Paul and me and put an arm around each of us.

"So," she began is if she might be starting a cross-examination in court, "does the darling Eric know anything about this?"

Oh god, Eric. How could I have put him out of my mind? As I sat there between my two best friends in the whole world, I had begun to feel a false sense of security. I knew Eric well enough to know that when (not if) I told him about the books, it would change everything. My life would never be the same. I wasn't sure I was really ready for that despite my misgivings about my lifestyle choices.

It occurred to me that tonight might not be the best time to break the news. I made a decision that I would, though, and soon. But just not right this moment.

SIXTEEN

It seemed that the activities in the swimming pool were now drawing to a close – as was the party. I checked my watch and found that it was already 1 am: high time the guests of honor said good-bye and thanked their hosts for a lovely evening.

There's something about hot, sticky summer-like evenings. Ever since childhood, I had believed that all manner of peculiar things would happen, especially during summer solstice. I was thinking about sunrise at Stonehenge, wondering if that experience might change someone's life forever. There was no doubt that this particular summer solstice would go down in the history of my life as a watershed.

I watched the bedraggled-looking guests file past Rebecca and David, offering them thanks and wishing them a good night. Jonathan, J.B., MacDonald was among those departing guests, but wasn't quite as dishevelled as the others since he had chosen not to take a midnight dip in the pool. His wife had clearly made the same decision. What was odd, though, was that the two of them were standing in the foyer talking to, of all people, Robert and Renée. They seemed to be deep in

227

conversation. I wondered how Robert was going to be able to face his senior partner after the consequences of his actions had been discovered by everyone – which they most assuredly would be. Life would never be the same for any of them, either.

Eric on the other hand was nowhere to be found. It occurred to me that I still had not discovered what he was up to this evening – what had brought on such uncharacteristic behavior. At least I might be able to get out of here before he started baring his soul to someone. Then I saw him.

He was standing in the living room talking to a water-soaked young man whom I did not recognize – yet another one. Under Eric's left arm he seemed to be holding a laptop. Strange, I thought. Rebecca emerged from the dining room, seeming to have rid herself of her mother at least temporarily. She turned, scanned the room and fixed her gaze directly on me. I felt distinctly uncomfortable although I hadn't the slightest notion why I should.

I looked around. Robert and Renée had made their way back into the living room, as had David and Sandy. Isobel and Paul stood just outside the archway looking as if they wanted to leave. Myra then lumbered into the room wearing a fresh caftan. She looked around as if trying to find Rebecca who was hiding behind Renée. Most of the rest of the guests seemed to have left.

228

Eric put down his drink, looked round at the remaining group and started in my direction. He was clearly drunk, but seemed to be trying desperately not to give away the extent of his inebriation. He slowly and carefully placed the laptop on the table, and then plugged in a flash drive. He opened a file then turned to me.

"Alex, darling, perhaps you'd like to tell us all a story," he said carefully, trying not to slur his words.

"Why should I tell anyone a story?" I was starting to feel that prickle of apprehension that so often started in the nape of my neck.

"Well, you're probably the most experienced story-teller here, aren't you?"

"Eric, you're drunk and talking nonsense." I was the one who needed a drink. This was not going well.

"Let me try to make sense, then," he said looking around at his audience as if to determine if they were, indeed, paying attention. He continued. "I have placed before you on the table an electronic file. It's not just any electronic file. It's a special file, and I think that you will all be quite shocked to find out what's in the file."

Everyone was looking very confused, that is, everyone except Isobel and Paul who looked more alarmed than confused.

Eric evidently had not finished his speech. "I happened to find this file on my wife's own laptop this morning. It puzzled me at first, but then I started to do a bit of investigation. It's been a rather enlightening day to say the least.

It struck me like a bolt of lightning. My laptop. On my dresser. With Paul's email winking at me – and my edited manuscript attached. I hadn't logged out and turned off the computer before I took a shower to get ready for the party. Eric must have found it.

"Ladies and gentlemen, I hope that none of you ever have to find out that the one person in the world that you thought you could trust has been keeping a secret from you. Not any little secret, like how much money she spent on those weird, purple shoes. I'm talking about a life-changing secret. I'm talking about a wife who's leading a double life."

"Eric," I said, "I don't think this is the time or the place for this. Let's go home. Whatever it is you're on about, we can talk about it there – in private." I was almost whispering, hoping that he was the only one who could hear me.

"*Au contraire*, my dear. I believe that this is both the time and the perfect place. This discussion needs to take place in the presence of witnesses."

What could he possibly mean by that last remark? Was he planning some kind of legal antic?

Was he going to demand a divorce right here in front of everyone?

He gestured toward the computer screen. "On that computer is evidence that my wife leads a sordid double life. It is clear that she cares not a scintilla for her husband of ten years." Then he turned to me. "I suppose you left your email open this afternoon so that I'd find it. Don't you think that's a tad cowardly – leaving it out for me to find instead of telling me? How long has this been going on?"

I looked over at Paul and Isobel who both seemed to be rather enjoying this in a peculiar kind of way.

"I'm not exactly sure what you think has been 'going on' as you put it."

"Then let me enlighten you while I enlighten our dear friends." He lifted the laptop from the table as if to show the screen to everyone.

I was reminded of executioners holding up decapitated heads after the striking of the guillotine in movies depicting the French Revolution. I sighed and said nothing. *We might as well get this over with*, I thought.

"When I arrived home from work today, tired from a hard day and looking forward to a lovely evening with our closest friends, I found this. Now, I'm not in the habit of reading my wife's private email, but something, God perhaps, made me do it today. I think that God actually spoke to me."

Well, that was one justification for invading someone's privacy. I had always known that Eric had fundamentalist Christian tendencies, but this was getting spooky – God spoke to him? Good lord. Could this get any weirder?

"This file, friends, contains the products of a mind that is seriously dysfunctional. It seems to be the product of a secret libidinal passion hidden deep inside a mind that cannot live in the real world."

The real world? He was starting to sound like some kind of demented preacher.

"In some sense I am relieved that you have chosen to keep this filth a secret. My only relief in all of this is that these books that you have clearly penned are relatively unknown." He gestured toward me with a flourish. "Ladies and gentlemen, I give you J.L. Kidston, writer of pornography."

Neither Isobel nor Paul could keep their giggles under control any longer. Eric looked daggers at them. He looked truly maniacal. Finally Paul spoke.

"Well, Dr. Harvey, I don't think you've done your homework as well as you think you have. If you'd permit me?" He walked over to the laptop which Eric had placed back on the table. He clicked a few times and then turned the screen toward Eric.

"There you are, sir. I just searched for J.L. Kidston. Can you read how many hits?"

Eric was peering closely at the screen, a look of incredulity on his face.

"That's right," Paul said. "J. L. Is one of the most prolific and popular writers of women's fiction – strike that – erotica, not pornography, on the planet. She has over two million Twitter followers and has sold – well, let's just say she's sold a lot of books." He looked at me. "And many more to come, I hope."

"Who exactly are you, anyway?" Rebecca said to Paul.

"I'm proud to say that I'm J.L.'s editor – I mean Alex's editor."

Rebecca looked dumbfounded. "Wow!" was all she could manage.

"Please don't tell me you've ever read any of this filth," Eric said to Rebecca.

"Well, as a matter of fact…"

"As a matter of fact," David interjected, "correct me if I'm wrong Becca, but there are at least three of her books on your bedside table." He looked at her tenderly. "I know why. I'm sorry." Then he turned to me. "And bravo to you, Alex. I didn't know, but to tell you the truth, I'm not entirely surprised. You always did seem a bit out of step with the rest of us. Thank-you for your work."

233

Eric looked as if he had been struck. As he gathered himself together he said, "Well, Alex or J. L. or whatever your name is, what do you have to say about all of this?"

I thought for a moment before I spoke. "I'm not sure what else I can say. You seem to have said it all. I am who I am. I'm sorry I couldn't share this with you, but I could not. I know you well enough to know that you could never have understood, and I was right."

"Don't you care what other people will say about you now?"

"To tell you the truth, Eric, it's been a long time since I've cared about that at all. I don't care what anyone thinks of what I do, what I say, what I wear, what I drive, what I eat or whom I consort with. And I don't care if kimchee is the in thing, I hate it!" I was just getting warmed up.

"I've spent the past ten years of my life trying to figure out why it is that you do care so damn much about these things."

Eric opened his mouth to speak, but I wasn't finished yet.

"You know, it's funny," I said, warming to my audience and topic, "most of the characters in my books which some of you," I looked directly at Eric, "hold in such disdain, have more real lives and authentic experiences than any of you, with the possible exception of Paul and Isobel."

234

"And me." Aunt Myra was beaming. A fan, perhaps?

I continued. "I don't know if you realize it or not, but you have contempt for anyone who doesn't share your love of the Yuppie lifestyle. I mean, who but a Yuppie would wait in line for two hours to sit at crappy benches for pizza just because someone says it's the 'in' thing to do. And don't get me started on all that expensive organic stuff in our refrigerator."

Everyone seemed speechless. I looked around at the faces. Only Paul and Isobel seemed happy – David and Sandy only a little less so.

"I must confess," I said continuing, "I have been a dismal failure at the lifestyle so many of our so-called friends seem to hold so dear. Everything is so predictable. It seems that I'm not the only one however, who is leading a kind of double life. Well, at least I'm claiming it now." I was now talking directly to Eric. "By the way, everyone is going to get old someday. All the working out and plastic surgery in the world won't change that. There is only one thing I know for sure: everything in life has a beginning, a middle and an end. And this is the end of one thing."

A solitary, slow clapping began. It was soon joined by another, then another. I looked at Paul who had started the applause. "The beginning of something new means that you can set up a photo shoot. It's time my readers knew what I look like."

"You can't possibly mean that the world will now know that my wife is the purveyor of such smut."

"Don't worry, Eric," I said over my shoulder as I headed out the door. "You will never have to be known as the husband of such a writer." He still didn't get it at all.

Olivia knew that she really did have to go home now. Her real home. Not the penthouse in the sky with the limousine driver waiting at the curb. Not the life where she chose her sexual partners like she chose her shoes from her walk-in closet the size of a small bungalow. No, her real home. But first, one more ride in the limo. Her chauffeur took her hand, helping her to slide into the softness of the buttery leather. She sat back and burrowed her face into the sable collar of her coat. The limousine made its way silently through the night streets that were wet from an earlier rain shower. Olivia took a sip of champagne from the crystal flute and felt her eyes fluttering closed. As the limo entered the tunnel, sleep was upon her. In her dream she found herself standing in a tunnel peering at the speck of crystalline light that was but a pinprick at the other end. Otherwise she was in complete darkness. She moved toward the light. The closer she got, the
236

warmer it made her feel as if she were lying naked in the tropical sunlight, a gentle breeze caressing her skin. Slowly she made her way toward the light. Was she near death? Had she completed her journey on earth? She reached the end of the tunnel and took a step into the light. At once she felt she had made a mistake. She was falling, like Alice falling down the rabbit hole. Would she ever stop falling?

Olivia woke up with a start and looked around. Where was she? She was no longer in the limousine. She was in bed. But whose bed? She got up and walked around the room, touching all of the objects just to be sure it was real. She touched the pillows first, then the old alarm clock on the night stand. The time said 5:30. She picked up the pair of eye glasses on the nightstand, and put them on, instinctively knowing they were hers. They improved the view. She walked toward the closet. As she opened the door, she began touching the clothes hanging inside. She touched the suits, the blouses, the pumps, the sensible walking shoes and hunted in vain for a mink coat. It wasn't there. She walked over to the window. She placed her palm on the glass. It felt cold. Snow was falling lightly on the shrubs two stories below and onto the little Volkswagen Beetle that sat in the driveway. Where was the limo?

She looked over at the bed. She had missed it entirely. There beside where she had just been asleep ws a man. He looked familiar. She walked over and stood there looking down at him. It was Jack. He was her husband. She was home.

EPILOGUE

Readers hate epilogues, but I need one.

My tenth wedding anniversary was indeed a watershed for me – and for a lot of other people, it has to be said. That was eighteen months ago, but in some ways it seems like it all happened to someone else.

Once I was settled in my new apartment, I took another look at the manuscript for *Reverie for a Solitary Night*. Paul had made some suggestions for changes and this time I was seriously considering them. I had been living with Olivia in my head for longer than I had kept other characters. It wasn't enough for her to have just let go of her fantasy, Paul told me. She had to have changed somehow as a result of it. So I rewrote the ending.

Olivia decided to change her life. Just because it was only a dream, didn't mean that the message should be ignored. She took a long, hard look at her life and decided to make changes. She began by taking a long, hard look at her marriage. In the end, she realized that the life she was leading didn't reflect who she was becoming, so Jack had to go. Next, she embarked on a personal make-over something like the narcissistic *Eat, Pray, Love* triumvirate. When she emerged from that

239

makeover, she was more similarly aligned with the Olivia in her dream. That's when life really began. She met the love of her life on an island in the Bahamas and the rest is history – with lots of sex thrown in!

That was my cross-over book. No longer was J.L. Kidston hiding behind a fake persona, not sticking strictly to women's erotica. She branched out. My next book is a big one and what's truly exhilarating for me is that my name is going to be on the cover. Mine! Alex Landers (I dropped Eric's last name when I dropped him from my life.) If it sounds familiar, it is. Landers-Pearson was the company I worked for. The Landers part was my father – oops! Didn't tell you that, did I? Yes, I worked for Dad, but I don't any longer. He thought it best if I took on my new writer's persona fully and left the account directing to others. I agreed. But he also told me to take back my name. So I did.

Six months ago I married Paul on a beach in Barbados with Isobel and her new husband at our side. He's still my editor, though. As I think back on that fateful evening, I can see that it was inevitable. The secrets had to come out one way or another. Of all the confessions that I heard, though, Eric's was the saddest. He had nothing to hide. I think that he is the dullest man I have ever known.

After all is said and done, there is one thing that I know to be true. Despite reports to the contrary, Yuppies will never die out.

ABOUT PATRICIA PARSONS

After twenty years of health & business writing, including authoring or co-authoring 11 books and numerous articles, Patricia Parsons took her first bold step into creative non-fiction with the publication in 2009 of her memoir *Another 'Pointe' of View: The Life and Times of a Ballet Mom* (Dreamcatcher Publishing), a book that chronicled her unexpected life as the mother of an elite ballet dancer – all the more surprising in a hockey-mad country like Canada, since that dancer is her son.

Following up on that experience, she took her considerable research skills to her second passion: historical fiction and women's fiction. She is the author of the novels *Grace Note: In Hildegard's Shadow* and *In the Shadow of the Raven*.

By day, she is a Professor of Communication Studies at a small, east coast university.

Connect with her on her web site at
www.patriciajparsons.com
or on Twitter @pparsons07

www.ingramcontent.com/pod-product-compliance
Lightning Source LLC
Chambersburg PA
CBHW020321200626
46814CB00006BB/2359